"Isn't that why I'm here?" But it still took a lot of nerve for her to actually come out and say it. "Because you can teach me."

Alessio frowned. "Teach you what?"

"Everything you know." She shrugged. "About sex. Think about it, Alessio," she challenged softly. "You're experienced and I'm not—but I've always been an excellent student."

His face was a picture. There was desire—yes, but it was the flicker of uncertainty in his eyes that made him seem more human. More accessible. And that was dangerous. She couldn't possibly make such a cold-blooded demand if she was then going to commit the cardinal crime of falling in love with him. There was no point in being bold and ambitious if she then came over as vulnerable.

But he had recovered his equilibrium and his faint consternation had been replaced by a slow smile of anticipation which was making her tummy tighten. "You want me to teach you everything I know about sex, do you, *cara*?" he murmured. "It's certainly the most unconventional request I've ever received from a woman but rest assured, Nicola—it will be my pleasure."

Sharon Kendrick once won a national writing competition by describing her ideal date: being flown to an exotic island by a gorgeous and powerful man. Little did she realize that she'd just wandered into her dream job! Today she writes for Harlequin, and her books feature often stubborn but always to-die-for heroes and the women who bring them to their knees. She believes that the best books are those you never want to end. Just like life...

Books by Sharon Kendrick

Harlequin Presents

Cinderella's Christmas Secret
One Night Before the Royal Wedding
Secrets of Cinderella's Awakening
Confessions of His Christmas Housekeeper
Her Christmas Baby Confession
Innocent Maid for the Greek

Jet-Set Billionaires

Penniless and Pregnant in Paradise

Passionately Ever After...

Stolen Nights with the King

Visit the Author Profile page at Harlequin.com for more titles.

Sharon Kendrick

ITALIAN NIGHTS TO CLAIM THE VIRGIN

HARLEQUIN®
PRESENTS™

PLEASE RECYCLE
THIS PRODUCT IS RECYCLABLE

Recycling programs
for this product may
not exist in your area.

ISBN-13: 978-1-335-73936-0

Italian Nights to Claim the Virgin

Copyright © 2023 by Sharon Kendrick

For questions and comments about the quality of this book, please contact us at CustomerService@Harlequin.com.

Harlequin Enterprises ULC
22 Adelaide St. West, 41st Floor
Toronto, Ontario M5H 4E3, Canada
www.Harlequin.com

Printed in U.S.A.

ITALIAN NIGHTS TO CLAIM THE VIRGIN

This story was inspired by Il Giardinello, the Umbrian home of my dearest friends, Guy Black and Mark Bolland.

In this exquisite setting I have enjoyed countless laughs and good times—delicious food, lively debate and stunning sunsets.

Grazie, cari! xxx

PROLOGUE

ALESSIO DI BARI COULD cope with the fact that Nicola Bennett disliked him. He was used to women disliking him—usually when they finally realised he had no intention of budging from his negative position on matrimony, or indeed any form of long-term commitment.

And he was used to anger. Hot-blooded passion, which often ended up in the bedroom in a riot of hastily discarded clothing and warm, pulsating flesh. It made a welcome change from his infamously cold and scientific demeanour.

What he wasn't used to was indifference.

He frowned, because such a lukewarm sentiment was insulting—and it was definitely indifference which was filtering through the air towards him as he stood within the airy confines of the exclusive London art gallery.

'Would you like some coffee, Signor di Bari?'

Her eyes were glacial, he thought. Cool as ice. But

then, everything about Nicola Bennett was cool. Her clothes. Her demeanour. Even her voice—every syllable carefully chipped out, as if she'd thought about each and every word she was uttering.

Alessio met the shuttered grey gaze which gleamed from her unmoving features, puzzled by his fascination for her. Because she certainly wasn't beautiful and neither was she particularly well-dressed—although he recognised that he had fairly exacting standards. Her plain white shirt and plain black skirt were undeniably smart but surely a little *dull*. Her shoes were sensible, *sì*, as were her neatly filed fingernails—but again, they were dull. Her only adornment was the thinnest gold chain he had ever seen—a modest piece of jewellery which glittered at the base of her long neck. Her pale hair was styled into a neat pleat at the back of her head and, because he had never seen a single strand of it out of place, he sometimes thought it looked more like a helmet. Nothing *feminine* about such a style as that, he thought disparagingly. Indeed, the only thing which marred her neat precision was the tiny rose-shaped birthmark on one side of her breastbone.

She was the most uptight woman he had ever met.

A pulse at his temple flickered.

Very uptight.

Yet at times, didn't he find his gaze inexplicably straying to that rosy little birthmark and wondering what her skin would taste like if he traced its raised surface with the tip of his tongue? Or imagine how it might be if he unclipped that severe hairstyle and let the blonde strands tumble in silken profusion over his fingers?

Again, he frowned.

What was *that* all about?

And since he was a scientist and therefore a man who abhorred the grey landscape of uncertainty, he always demanded answers to speculative questions. Perhaps it was because his busy schedule had been off the scale recently, with a new factory opening in Germany as well as another in his adopted country of America. But the subsequent stream of late nights and early mornings had led to an almost complete absence of leisure. Was it that which was responsible for him fantasising about the most unlikely of people, like the cool Miss Nicola Bennett?

'Shouldn't you be offering me champagne?' he drawled. 'Considering the significant hole which has blasted its way through my finances as a result of purchasing this overpriced painting.' He raised his eyebrows as he gestured towards the large canvas. 'Wouldn't you have thought your boss would have presented me with a hefty discount for being such a regular customer to his gallery, considering we've been friends for so long?'

But her implacable features barely moved and her polite smile stayed frozen in place. 'If you wait until the weekend, you'll get the chance to haggle with him in person,' she answered smoothly. 'He's due back from Argentina on Friday.'

'Unfortunately, I'm busy at the weekend,' said Alessio, but when he thought about the reason why, he could feel a trickle of distaste whisper over his skin.

'Oh, that's a shame.' She gave a small shrug, which rather distractingly drew his attention to the slender curve of her breasts, which were outlined in crisp white cotton. 'For what it's worth, I happen to think you've got yourself a bargain,' she added.

'Do you?'

'Of course.'

Silently, their gazes travelled to the oil painting which depicted a woman sitting beside a bathtub, wearing nothing but a man's shirt and the expression of someone who had just been sexually satisfied. Her dark hair was tangled, her thighs slightly open and a soft smile was playing at the edges of her lips. The artist was well known for portraits of his many lovers and it was an astonishing piece of work, yet there was something about the study which was uncomfortably intimate, which made the viewer feel almost like a voyeur.

Alessio couldn't imagine staring at a woman for long enough to paint her in such a situation—even if he possessed a shred of artistic ability, which he definitely didn't. He was the type of man who cut short post-coital reflection by going straight to the bathroom and dousing himself beneath the jets of a powerful shower and afterwards becoming engrossed in work—employing any method he could to avoid sentimental contemplation. It had been noted and complained about on more than one occasion, but he had no intention of changing his behaviour. Why should he?

He glanced at the smooth profile of the woman beside him, noting the faint flush of colour which was staining her creamy skin as she studied the painting. 'Do you like it?' he enquired.

'It's one of his finest pieces of work,' she replied carefully.

'That's not what I asked, Nicola.' He paused, his gaze flickering over her. 'You're a very evasive woman, aren't you?'

'Am I?' She raised a pair of neat eyebrows. 'That's news to me. I just happen to prefer landscapes, Signor di Bari, nothing more mysterious than that.'

'And you never call me Alessio,' he observed softly. 'Even though I've asked you to on more than one occasion.'

There was a pause.

'Because I prefer professional boundaries,' she answered crisply. 'I refer to all Sergio's clients using their titles and nobody's ever objected before. In fact, some people seem to enjoy the use of formality in an increasingly informal age.'

Her accompanying smile made her words seem

light—almost flippant, but they were not flippant. They were... He narrowed his eyes. They were dismissive. *Sì*. Definitely dismissive. And so was she. He saw the way she glanced at her wrist, even though she was trying to disguise it by fiddling with the cuff of her white shirt, as if she were doing nothing more than innocently checking that the button was secure, rather than looking to see the time.

She was bored, he realised incredulously. And she wanted him gone. Alessio could feel a pulse thudding at his temple as a warm flame of anger heated his blood. Because for a moment it had felt as if Miss Cool was judging him, and that pressed all the wrong buttons to someone who had spent much of his life being judged. It took a moment for the feeling to pass and he gave an impatient shake of his head.

What was the *matter* with him? Since when had he started caring about what some unknown English shopgirl thought, and allowed it to impact his mood? She was nothing to him. Pity his poor friend Sergio Cabrera, who was forced to study her chilly countenance day after day. Pity even more her boyfriend. His lips hardened. That was if any man would be capable of enduring the company of such a cold fish as she.

'Have the painting shipped to my Manhattan address, would you?' he clipped out, pulling out his phone to direct his chauffeur to pick him up from the Mayfair gallery.

'With pleasure,' she answered politely.

Alessio couldn't help thinking that a woman like this would surely be a stranger to pleasure. He certainly couldn't imagine her showing it. Why, a plank of wood would display more emotion than Nicola Bennett!

And speaking of pleasure...

He thought about the evening ahead and the plea made by a man who'd been pivotal during the construction of the latest di Bari factory. Karl Schneider was young and dynamic, determined to see as much of London's nightlife as he could during his brief stay in the capital. Last night had been all about the theatre and dinner at an award-winning restaurant, but tonight...

Tonight was something which needed to be endured. Alessio wasn't crazy about Soho, or nightclubs—and old-school drinking establishments staffed by partially clothed women were definitely *not* his thing. He sighed. But he would go along with it because business was business and he liked Karl.

Maybe the place would surprise him and prove to be the one bright spot in a week over which a heavy black cloud was looming. He had no desire to attend his mother's birthday party, but this was one of the few occasions in his adult life when he felt as if he had no choice—an unwelcome acknowledgement for a man for whom control had always been key.

With a brief nod to the cool blonde who was opening the door for him, he swept from the gallery towards his waiting limousine and slid onto the back seat. He wondered just what form the forthcoming 'celebration' would take. And he wondered just how bad it was going to be.

A ragged sigh left his lungs.

A whole weekend to endure, with nobody but his toxic family for company.

CHAPTER ONE

THE SUMMER RAIN was torrential. It splashed up the back of Nicola's calves and dripped back down into her shoes, making them squelch as she walked. Already she was soaked to the skin and her flimsy umbrella was proving useless against the driving wind. Also, she was cold and very hungry and these were the factors which should have been her sole focus this evening, especially as she had a long shift ahead of her.

But it wasn't just that she hadn't had time to sit down and eat before coming here—all Nicola could think about was Alessio di Bari. No matter how hard she tried she couldn't seem to shift his image from her mind, or block out the memory of his mocking, silken voice.

She'd often thought he was a bit of a contradiction. His appearance did nothing to suggest he was a highly successful chemist, with factories dotted around the globe—and most people agreed that he looked more like a movie star than a scientist. He possessed a dark and sensual beauty which made her go to pieces every time he walked into the London art gallery where she'd worked for the past three years, often with a beautiful woman hanging onto his arm—although not lately, she noted. Gorgeous sensual creatures with legs up to their armpits and amazing boobs, often dripping with diamonds, which the Italian billionaire had probably lavished on them.

Nicola had never seen or met anyone like him. He exemplified power and strength and intellect. She'd seen the way people turned to look at him and she totally understood why—and it had nothing to do with his expensive suits or chauffeur-driven cars or private jets. But she hated the way he managed to storm his way into her thoughts, like some sexy, heat-seeking missile. Just as she hated his effect on her—although a lifetime of keeping her emotions hidden meant she was confident he had no idea about her feelings for him. She always put up her defences whenever he was around—yet somehow he managed to knock them down without trying, leaving her aching and vulnerable in a way which felt exciting, scary and unfamiliar.

She swallowed as his hard, chiselled features swam into her mind. Those bright sapphire eyes, set in skin of burnished gold. That mane of ebony hair which framed his face and that honed, muscular body, which no amount of handmade tailoring could disguise. Yet he had a particular skill in looking down his nose at her and Nicola resented him for that. Her carefully maintained poise always threatened to desert her whenever Alessio di Bari was around. She found herself wanting to touch him. To kiss him. To press his hard body close to hers and never let him go.

How insane was that?

Especially since she was that embarrassing thing which nobody of her age should be.

A virgin.

Snapped out of her thoughts by a buzzing sound from the depths of her handbag, Nicola sighed. She didn't have to look at her phone to know who was calling, which was why she chose not to ignore it. With a shiver, she sheltered underneath the dripping awning of a shop selling vintage comics and pulled out the vibrating handset.

'Nicky?' whined a familiar voice.

'Hello, Mum. Look, I can't talk for long. I've got to go to work. What's up?'

'It's Stacey.'

Of course it was. It was always Stacey. As ever, Nicola's heart plummeted at the mention of her brother's girlfriend. 'She's okay, isn't she?' she questioned urgently.

'Suppose so.' The deep inhalation of a cigarette was followed by a brief, rasping cough. 'Says she's fed up with the weather and thinking of going to Majorca. Apparently her auntie's got a time-share out there and says she can get her a job in some fancy café on the beachfront.'

Nicola bit back the obvious response that an eight months pregnant young woman with a lifelong aversion to work was unlikely to walk straight into a jammy job abroad—even if she could get a work permit sorted out in time, which Nicola doubted.

Clearing her throat, she attempted to project an air of calm. 'Mum, listen. Tell her everything's going to be okay. I've got some money I've been saving up for her and the baby and she's going to get it very soon.'

'She knows that. She wants to know why she can't have it. Now.' Another rasping cough. 'Says she needs furniture.'

Nicola bit her lip in frustration—because delayed gratification was as alien a concept to her mother as it was to her brother's girlfriend. She thought about Stacey's penchant for expensive make-up and handbags. Her love of eating out, which went hand in hand with an inability to cook anything more complicated than a piece of toast. 'I know she does, but I'm scared she'll fritter it away before the baby's born,' she confided huskily. 'Look, I'll go and visit her tomorrow and see what I can do. I'll reassure her and try to talk some sense into her, but I've got to go now, Mum, or I'll be late for work.'

She cut the connection and hurried across the shiny pavements which reflected the garish lights of the Soho streets, which were unusually quiet tonight—presumably because of the foul weather. At last she came to a halt in front of the Masquerade club—its pink neon lights flashing flamingo-bright alongside a giant photo of a canal and a gondola. A bouncer stood outside, mostly turning people away because this was the current hot ticket in town and the difficulty of gaining entry was one of the things which made it so attractive.

One of the doormen nodded as Nicola entered, slipping through a discreet interior door at the back and taking the stairs to the staff changing room in the basement, where she proceeded to get changed. It always took longer to put on her outfit than to remove the clothes she'd arrived in and there was a reason for that. Try as she could to break the habit, her movements were always reluctant because this costume was the last thing she would ever have chosen to wear. In fact, if she didn't need the money so desperately she would never have taken a job like this. But it was relatively easy and, more importantly, the tips were excellent—and that was what had kept her here for the last five months, laboriously putting aside every penny she earned.

Pulling her blonde hair from its neat pleat and shaking it free, Nicola peered into the mirror. The club was supposed to be Venice-themed, which was why the menu was full of *cicchetti* and bottles of expensive Valpolicella and barmen dressed in stripey tops with distinctive hats tipped at jaunty angles. While the waitresses, of which she was one...

She sighed. No way would her appearance offend anyone's sense of decency. There was more substance to her costume than something you might see on the beach—it was just so ridiculously *tight*. Her breasts felt as if they wanted to burst right out of the sequined bodice and her tiny skirt of black and purple feathers left far too much of her fishnet-covered thighs on show. And as for her shoes...

She glanced down at the killer stilettos. Her shoes were crazy-high. At least the traditional Venetian mask meant nobody would be able to recognise her, which had been another of the job's enticements—not that she knew anyone who would be prepared to pay these kinds of over-inflated prices for glasses of mediocre wine.

Going back upstairs, she picked up her tray and her electronic ordering pad and, walking into the dimly lit interior of the club, looked around. It was the usual selection of guests and they were nearly all men. Out-of-town visitors. A smattering of celebrities. A clutch of premier league footballers with a bevy of beautiful blondes hanging onto their every word.

The light on her electronic pad was flashing, instructing her to go to table thirteen—somewhat ironically numbered since it was the most prestigious table in the VIP section of the club. Nicola pinned a wide smile to her lips and swayed her hips, the way the manageress had taught her to, though the sky-scraper heels made the movement feel very exaggerated and secretly she wondered if it didn't make her look rather ridiculous. But her smile froze the instant she saw the two men who were sitting on the raised dais. Or rather, when she clocked the one who was gazing rather moodily at the empty dance floor, his hard profile drawing the covert and not so covert attention of pretty much every woman in the place. Beneath her too-tight bodice, her heart squeezed out a painful beat and her skin grew clammy and cold.

It couldn't be.

It couldn't.

Fate would never be that cruel, would it?

Yet she of all people should know how cruel fate could be. Of course it was him. Who else would it be? Because if anyone was going to walk in and discover her secret job—wouldn't it have to be the man she hated and fancied more than anyone in the world? Who just happened to be one of the best friends of her powerful boss...

Her heart began to race, because her boss, Sergio Cabrera, was in many ways a highly conservative man—it was one of the reasons he'd taken her on as Chief Assistant in his London art gallery in the first place. He approved of her prim, neat image and the fact that she never came to work with a hangover or allowed her love life—which was non-existent anyway—to impinge on work. Wouldn't he hit the roof if he discovered that his loyal and supposedly very conventional assistant was spending her evenings draped in minuscule scraps of feathers and lace, selling overpriced glasses of champagne to wealthy punters?

He mustn't find out. And the only way he could would be if Alessio recognised her and told him—so she must make sure that didn't happen.

She needed to stay calm. The Italian billionaire wouldn't look at her face. They never did. And even if he did—*even if he did*—she was wearing a mask, wasn't she? An elaborate sequinned mask which had the ability to conceal most of her features. She even thought about slipping back into the rough South London accent of her youth, which she'd tried to leave behind—but something inside her baulked at that. She had come too far to ever go back—and wasn't there a bit of her which felt that if she did, she would be swallowed up by the horrors of the past all over again?

Anyway, Alessio wouldn't have a clue it was her. Why would he? She doubted he would have given her a second thought after leaving the gallery today—let alone remember her. Someone like her wouldn't even register on his radar. She would take his order and deliver it as quickly as possible, averting her eyes all the time. Then ask one of the other waitresses if they wouldn't mind swapping sections for the rest of her shift.

But her fingers were trembling and her heart was still pounding beneath her tight costume as she weaved her way through the tables towards the two men. And then, making sure she addressed the man who wasn't Alessio, she said quietly, 'What can I get for you, sir?'

Alessio wasn't really concentrating as the blonde waitress took their order and neither was he particularly engaged when she returned to the table with a bottle of rosé champagne, even though he could remember his companion only asking for two glasses of the stuff.

But he frowned as he watched her tear pink foil from the neck of the bottle, his attention caught by the way her thumbs began to ease out the cork, thinking how long her fingers were and how incongruous her sensibly filed fingernails seemed in comparison to her flamboyant outfit. He wasn't sure what made his eyes travel upwards, past the badge which said 'Nicky', past the creamy thrust of her cleavage to her long neck—his gaze stopping to alight on a tiny birthmark on her neck, shaped like a rose.

Something flickered in the depths of his memory. *Shaped like a rose.*

She was focussing intently on the bottle, which she must have shaken because it had started to foam in a creamy cascade in a way which was exceedingly erotic. He could see her hand trembling as she splashed—yes, splashed—champagne into two tall goblets, but despite the mess she was making of the table, she was determinedly refusing to meet his gaze.

He could have let her go.

Maybe he should have let her go.

But his curiosity was stirred—which was rare—and so was something else. Something which felt like a fierce shaft of recognition and something else, too, something which felt uncomfortably like desire.

'Nicola?' he said softly. 'Is that really you?'

She lifted her gaze at last, and the eyes which met his were not so cool now, her glacial gaze melting into one of apprehension.

'Would there be any point in me denying it?' she said, her tone not quite as clipped as usual.

For a moment Alessio was so taken aback that he didn't answer. But it was less his shock at discovering her in such a bizarre setting which was responsible for his uncharacteristic hesitation, than the growing realisation that Nicola Bennett didn't usually do herself justice.

Not at all.

'I guess not,' he said slowly, his disbelieving gaze taking in her incredible body. 'Though it's proving a little difficult to get my head around. Seeing you here, like this.'

'I'm afraid I can't help you with that,' she said crisply as she began to mop up the spilt champagne. 'It is what it is.'

As she bent over the table her long hair swung like an armful of ripe corn—the coloured lights of the nightclub creating a neon kaleidoscope amid the thick and gleaming strands. Alessio's eyes narrowed, because he was baffled—and he was rarely baffled by a woman. He wondered why she hid that magnificent fall of hair—choosing instead that repressive helmet-like style which did her no favours. And why conceal that amazing body and achingly long legs beneath the type of clothes which made her look as if she'd taken a vow of chastity? For some bizarre reason he didn't actually *approve* of the skimpy outfit she was wearing tonight—but that didn't detract from the shimmering beauty she usually kept locked away.

Why did she do that?

His frown deepened.

And why the hell was she leading some sort of double life—working in a nightclub in an edgy part of the city, which was a world away from her sedate day job in privileged Mayfair?

She was staring at him—her grey eyes sending out a silent message which contained none of their usual enigma—as if daring him to interrogate her. And he wondered whether he might have done just that, if they hadn't been surrounded by other people, with the smoky note of a saxophone throbbing in the background, infiltrating the air with a layer of sensuality which only increased his feelings of disorientation.

'Hey, you two know each other, *ja*?'

Karl's voice broke the silence as he looked from one to the other of them—like somebody at a cocktail party waiting to be introduced—and Alessio responded with a lazy smile.

'We've met before,' he said carelessly. 'Though I wouldn't say we actually knew one another, would you, *Nicky*?'

He saw her throat work a little but that icy smile was back with all its chilly force.

'Not at all,' she said, with a quick smile. 'We've run into each other from time to time—but London is a much smaller city than people imagine, isn't it, Signor di Bari?' She stared at a spot in the far distance. 'Oh, look. Somebody over there is signalling for a drink. Will you excuse me?'

He watched her go. Long legs in fishnet tights and a provocative flurry of feathers which adorned a deliciously high bottom, and Alessio found himself captured by another achingly sweet shaft of a desire which had been absent from his life for too long now. And he couldn't just blame overwork. Wasn't it also to do with his innate sense of boredom and cynicism, because women came on to him all the time?

Because hadn't he reached the age of thirty-four with a sexual appetite which had lately grown very jaded?

He drank a mouthful of champagne, wincing at the inferior quality of the wine, before putting down the glass. He watched Nicola's elegant journey across the floor as she took the drinks order and then disappeared from the VIP section, instinctively knowing she had no intention of returning.

He wondered afterwards, if the dreaded weekend hadn't been approaching, whether he would have just let the matter lie. He could have stored the interesting and conflicting nugget of information about the cool Miss Bennett in the recesses of his mind, along with the many other of life's peculiarities which he'd picked up along the way.

But the weekend *was* approaching and he was increasingly focussed on what lay ahead. Various family members who hated one another—with a giant inheritance at stake, which exacerbated all the greed within his half-siblings which always simmered beneath the surface. If it hadn't been his mother's birthday he would have found an excuse to decline—but his refusal to attend would hurt her. And hadn't she been hurt enough during her foolish life?

He thought about the best strategy for coping with the ordeal. Perhaps he should have arranged to take a date with him but there was nobody he was interested in dating and it was too late now. What he needed was a woman who was suitably distracting, but who wouldn't get the wrong idea about his motives.

His lips curved into a hard smile because he'd suddenly had the most brilliant idea.

CHAPTER TWO

'HAVE DINNER WITH me tonight.'

Despite the drawled delivery of his statement, the velvety words were more of an order than an invitation, but somehow Nicola didn't react. She didn't imagine many women would've refused a dinner invitation from Alessio di Bari—but those women weren't her. Because presumably they had nothing to lose, while she had so much.

So very much.

Surveying him from the other side of the gallery, she thought—not for the first time—how incredible the human body was. Inside you could be experiencing a cocktail of dread and unwanted physical attraction, while on the outside she was aware of appearing as composed as she always did. All those relentless years of training hadn't let her down. At least, not so far, she thought grimly, meeting a pair of blue eyes so bright they looked almost electric—

which might account for the sparks which were fizzing over her skin.

Last night, she had worked the rest of her shift at the Masquerade club and although she had situated herself in the non-VIP section, she had been quaking with nerves, praying she wouldn't have to see Alessio again. And her prayers had been answered, because she hadn't.

When she'd peeped through the velvet curtain, he and his companion had no longer been there and she had heaved a great sigh of relief. He must have left soon after she'd served him the disgusting fizz they had the temerity to call champagne. He hadn't sought her out to say goodbye and she tried to convince herself she would hear no more about it. He would return to his fancy life in New York and next time he turned up to buy another painting—probably with another luscious brunette hanging off his arm—he would have forgotten all about it.

Yet when she'd arrived at work this morning, some gut instinct had warned her that the Italian billionaire wouldn't just let matters lie. Deep down she had suspected she would see him today—and she had been right. Shortly after eleven he had walked into the gallery, dressed in a charcoal suit which made him look impossibly cool and a pale shirt which was open at the neck. His black hair gleamed and he glowed with health, as if he'd just returned from a fortnight at a spa. She, on the other hand, was pasty and panda-eyed, having barely slept a wink all night.

But fear and trepidation would not serve her well in this situation. He had seen a side of her she had never intended him to see and somehow that removed the necessity to retreat behind the cool mask she always wore. It meant she was able to speak to him with a truth she would never have dared use previously.

'Why do you want to have dinner with me?' she said evenly. 'Are you planning to blackmail me?'

His evident surprise at her question did little to reassure her. Was that because the glint in his eyes remained as steely as ever?

'Blackmail you? *Madonna mia.'* Dark eyebrows were elevated in mocking query. 'You've been reading too many novels, *cara.'*

'I never read novels,' she replied repressively. 'I prefer facts.'

'Now why do I find that easy to believe? Although, actually, so do I,' he murmured.

'And is that relevant?'

'I guess not.' He gave a short laugh. 'Okay, Ms Prickly, I'll stick to facts. I would like very much to have a conversation with you.'

'Isn't that what we're doing right now?'

'Indeed we are. But another customer could easily walk in and interrupt us.'

'I might welcome an interruption.'

'And I might not.' He paused, and now the dazzling blue eyes were narrowed and determined. 'Nicola.'

Saying nothing, she waited for the inevitable.

'Or should I call you Nicky?'

Suddenly her hard-won aplomb drained away and Nicola felt herself grow tense. She could feel the approach of fear, because wasn't this like being back in the playground? And wasn't it disturbing how quickly those times could come flooding vividly back—as if the sophisticated veneer she had acquired over the years was melting away, like an ice cube in a warm drink? She remembered being the girl with holes in her shoes, her threadbare socks still damp from having washed them under the tap the night before. She remembered the tatty old lunchbox, which was always empty because she'd given her jam sandwiches to her hungry little brother.

But this was not the playground and she was no longer a schoolgirl—and even though this was the grown-up world, it could still be harsh and cruel. There was nobody to protect her now, just as there had been nobody to protect her then. Reflecting on the unfairness of life would get her nowhere—she needed to face the situation head-on and deal with it, same as she always had.

She knew that, in theory, there was nothing in her contract to say she couldn't get an evening job as a waitress—but she knew her boss would not be pleased. Because this was a world where image was everything. Crisp white blouses and neat black skirts were one thing—fishnet tights and feathery bottoms were a very different ballgame. That had been her choice and she had been found out, but she was damned if she was going to give up and buckle under—especially to *this* man.

She gave an exaggerated sigh. 'Look, why don't I save you the cost of a meal, Signor di Bari? If you want to tell Sergio about last night, than go ahead and tell him.' She shrugged. 'If he sacks me, he sacks me—I'll cope. There are always other jobs. But please don't start making veiled threats under the guise of asking me to dinner, because I can assure you that I'm not easy to intimidate.'

'Whoa! Easy!'

He was holding up his palms as if warding off an attack and the brief puzzlement on his granite features seemed genuine enough. And suddenly Nicola felt a rush of remorse—because that wasn't the most diplomatic way to speak to one of the gallery's best customers, was it? She had no right to be rude to him, just because she fancied him.

'Sorry,' she mumbled. 'I shouldn't have said that.'

'Do you always think the worst of people?' he questioned curiously.

She was tempted to tell him that yes, she did.

She'd had plenty of reason to—and experience was a brutal teacher. But nobody wanted to listen to a sob story—especially not a man like him, who had wealth and privilege dripping from every pore of his body. Ever since she'd entered the hallowed world of selling paintings which cost more than an average house, Nicola had discovered that rich men—and women—thought everything in their world should be perfect. Their money was supposed to protect them from the cares which ordinary people suffered. They wanted sparkle. Magic. Not some glorified shop assistant pouring out her woes.

'I do tend to be a glass-half-empty sort of person,' she concurred wryly. 'But I'm always pleasantly surprised when I'm proved wrong.'

'So let me prove you wrong,' he said softly. 'Have dinner with me.'

'Why?'

'Because I find you intriguing.'

'I can assure you, I'm not.'

'Modest, too,' he observed.

She stared at him, trying to tell herself she didn't care what he thought of her, but it was hard to deny the sudden heat of her blood. 'Why?' she repeated steadily.

There was a pause. 'Because I have a proposition which might be of interest to you. And I don't think this is the right time or the right place to tell you about it.'

'Now who's being intriguing?'

'I know.' His sensual lips curved into a smile. 'It's an irresistible quality, isn't it?'

Suspiciously, Nicola identified his deliberate switch to charm, which did nothing to mask the steely resolve underpinning his words. Because that was something else she'd discovered about rich people. They were used to getting what they wanted, *when* they wanted it and she suspected that Alessio di Bari wouldn't go away until he had got what he'd come in for.

She couldn't imagine what his *proposition* was, but would it really hurt to humour him? Maybe even pretend to be flattered to receive an invitation from him—as she imagined most women with a pulse would be. She could come up with some cock-and-bull story about why she was moonlighting in the West End. She could explain that she needed new furniture. Which was true. Maybe even persuade him to keep her little secret to himself, so that Sergio would be none the wiser. She smiled and now it was *her* turn to switch on the charm—another lesson she had learned from watching other people. She tried to smile with her eyes, the way she knew you were supposed to—even though sometimes her eyes felt as empty as dry wells.

'Okay, then,' she said. 'Where did you have in mind?'

'My driver will pick you up.' He pulled his phone from his pocket. 'Let me have your address.'

'No.' Nicola felt a sudden flicker of apprehension as she imagined this powerful man turning up at an apartment which barely had enough room for one person, let alone two. But it wasn't so much that she was ashamed of her home—more that she couldn't contemplate all his powerful charisma being contained in such a modest space. It would be like trying to trap a hurricane in a matchbox. 'I'll meet you at the restaurant.'

His blue eyes narrowed. 'Are you always this guarded?'

'Always,' she affirmed coolly, plucking an ivory card from the edge of the glass desk and handing it to him. 'Here's my card, with my number. Text me the name of the restaurant when you've booked it.'

Alessio took the card, the brief brush of her fingers making his pulse rate soar, and he wondered how such an innocent touch could feel so unbelievably *erotic*. Was it because he'd never had to work this hard to get a woman to agree to have dinner with him which made her so fascinating? Or because he couldn't shift the memory of the way she had looked last night, in her fishnet tights and feathery miniskirt with that cascade of blonde hair gleaming down her back, which was a world away from today's buttoned-up appearance?

Reluctantly, he heaved out a sigh. 'As you wish. Seven-thirty okay? I have an early flight in the morning.'

'Make it eight-thirty, would you?' she amended crisply.

'Are you always this...*difficult*, Nicola?'

'I'm not being difficult. I...' Some of her composure seemed to leave her. 'I have a few errands I need to run after work, that's all.'

Shopping most probably, he thought, with the sudden beat of satisfaction—rushing to the nearest store to buy a new dress in order to impress him. But his mood had soured by the time his car drew up outside the gallery, because coming second to a bunch of *errands* was a novel experience for him. He gave a hard smile. Still. Let her play her little games. He rather relished the idea of having someone to cross swords with. It would certainly make a change from his usual dates, most of whom had taken submission to a whole new level. Even the smartest of women seemed to spend spent an inordinate amount of time trying to gauge his mood. Trying to work out how to become...

What?

Indispensable?

Probably. And from there they imagined it was one short step to getting a wedding band on their finger and a baby in the crib.

But no woman was indispensable and no woman was ever going to become his wife, because marriage was a flawed institution and one he despised. Yet no matter how many times he repeated his distaste at the thought of commitment, every woman thought she could be the one to change his mind.

Maybe that was the real reason why he'd been celibate for almost a year now, aware that the recent publicity surrounding his elevation to the super-rich list had made him something of a marital quarry. And, *sì*, his body might sometimes ache with a sexual hunger which was fierce and raw, but in a way it had been liberating not to have to meet a pair of reproachful eyes over his breakfast coffee when he explained he was going away on business. Or having to explain why he couldn't possibly commit to Christmas, when it was only July.

He spent the rest of the day in meetings, but when he returned to his hotel to change before dinner, he couldn't deny the unfamiliar ripple of excitement which had little to do with the proposition he was about to put to the enigmatic Miss Bennett. Standing beneath the powerful jets of water, he could feel the heavy throb of desire.

Did she have a man in her life? he wondered idly as icy droplets rained over his heated skin. His hair still damp, he walked over to the hotel window with its sweeping views of Green Park, bright with flowers on this warm summer evening. But he wasn't really concentrating on the view. His thoughts were still preoccupied with Nicola. Because if she *was* seeing someone, there was the very real possibility she might turn him down, and that was unthinkable. Pulling a silk shirt from the wardrobe, he felt the whisper of silk cool against his flesh as he acknowledged that he found her a challenge.

And he couldn't remember the last time *that* had happened.

CHAPTER THREE

IT WASN'T WHAT Nicola had been expecting. A tiny restaurant in an unfashionable part of London, with a weathered sign which hung beneath the faded awning saying Marco's. She frowned as she checked her phone, wondering if she'd made a mistake. Whether the crazy thundering of her heart when she'd received Alessio's message had made her misread the text and brought her to a decidedly unflashy part of town. But no. This was definitely the right address.

So where were the neat bay trees standing sentry by the door? The bouncer discreetly keeping away the common people while making room for the press? Pushing open the door, she could hear the buzz of lively conversation as she stepped into a room to be instantly greeted by a beaming maître d'.

'Buona sera, signorina.'

'Good evening.' She gripped her clutch bag a little tighter. 'I'm meeting—'

'*Sì, sì.* I know exactly who you are meeting.' He gave a flourish of his hand. 'Come this way, *signorina.*'

Either the man was a mind-reader or Alessio had tipped him off, because she was being led past tables decked with old-fashioned red-and-white-checked tablecloths, adorned with small vases of plastic flowers—plastic!—towards a booth right at the back of the room. And Nicola felt her throat drying with a mixture of disbelief and longing, because there was Alessio di Bari, waiting for her. Waiting for *her.* It was like a scene from a film, or maybe a dream, and she could do nothing to prevent the sudden thundering of her heart. He was rising to his feet to greet her, looking impossibly gorgeous in a beautifully cut charcoal suit which defined the broadness of his shoulders, the long legs and narrow hips.

She tried not to feel nervous, but the truth was that she did—because this felt too much like a date and she'd given up on dates, a long time ago. Why had that been? she wondered fleetingly. When she'd realised that she didn't fit in anywhere? Not in the world she had left behind, nor the shiny new one she had embraced. When she'd accepted that on some level she had been disappointing the men who had taken her out for drinks, or dinner—because she wasn't what they expected. Despite her fancy job in one of London's most sophisticated galleries, she wasn't posh and she certainly hadn't been to the 'right' schools. She wasn't who she appeared to be from the outside.

And she could never let them know who she truly was.

But tonight definitely wasn't a date and it was perfectly okay to be nervous about what to wear, because she'd never been out with a man like Alessio before. In the end she had opted for an old but much-loved dress, which she had carefully maintained over the years. It had been very expensive and she had spent a long time saving up for it—but it was considered a 'classic', which wouldn't look out of place in even the fanciest of settings, and she'd certainly got a lot of wear out of it. Though judging by the rustic simplicity of the place she needn't have bothered— jeans would have fitted in much better.

Why was she even here, she thought crossly as she sat down, angsting about what to wear and wondering if she looked okay? Why had she docilely agreed to his request, instead of turning him down and calling his bluff? But as she placed her bag on the banquette she knew why—and it wasn't just because the Italian billionaire had discovered one of her secrets. Wasn't the truth a little more complicated? Hadn't the sheer force of his personality flattened her like a steamroller, so that she'd been unable to turn him down? And that was dangerous. *He* was dangerous.

'Nicola,' he said as he sat down opposite her. 'Thank you for coming.'

'I don't think I had a choice, do you?' she challenged pleasantly.

'I think we both know that's not true.'

'Whatever,' she said, with a careless shrug. But although this whole situation might not be to her liking, she couldn't deny the satisfaction she derived from this newfound freedom to speak to him exactly as she pleased.

In a rapid stream of Italian, he spoke to the maître d', who was hovering by his side, and, once the man had hurried away, he studied her from across the table. 'I've ordered for you. I hope you don't mind?'

She raised her brows. 'Why did you do that?'

'I didn't want to waste any time with protracted decision-making and I trust the staff's advice about what's the best thing on the menu.' He glittered her a look. 'Unless you have any allergies?'

'Only to arrogant men making decisions for me.'

'I can always call him back if you'd prefer something different.'

Nicola shook her head, though she wasn't quite as indignant as she would have him believe. Because she wasn't supposed to *like* a man behaving in such an outrageously masterful way. She was proud of her hard-won independence and his approach was so last century. So why was an unfamiliar softness beginning to unfurl deep inside her? Because it made a change to have someone else making a decision, or because his easy confidence made him seem even sexier?

She shook her head, sitting back against the banquette and looking around the room, which was preferable to losing herself in the brilliance of Alessio's electric-blue eyes. The place was almost full—mostly with young families—though there were several couples of differing ages. It was an understated place. Relaxed. People looked happy, she thought—as if they didn't have a care in the world—and suddenly she felt wistful. But she couldn't spend the whole evening looking everywhere except at Alessio and so, as the waiter poured wine and water, Nicola directed her gaze towards the carved contours of his beautiful face.

'This isn't a bit what I expected,' she said.

'No? Let me guess.' His hard blue gaze raked over her. 'Chandeliers and a hushed atmosphere? Waiters dressed like penguins and food which has been messed around with so much that it's unrecognisable?'

Biting back a reluctant smile, she shrugged. 'Something like that.'

'Formality and luxury have their place but so does this. They make the best home-made pasta outside Italy, which is why it's always full.' He lifted his glass, surveying her mockingly over its rim. 'Are you disappointed I didn't treat you to an evening of five-star excellence, Nicola?'

She watched him take a sip of wine, unwillingly fascinated by the gleam which highlighted his bottom lip, despairing at her sudden urge to drink in all his golden dark, masculine beauty. Because this wasn't why she was here. She wasn't supposed to be *flirting*. She shook her head. 'Not disappointed at all. I think it's a lovely place and very unpretentious.' She drew in a deep breath. 'But why don't we just cut to the chase? You obviously don't want to waste any time and neither do I. The venue is irrelevant. You still haven't told me why I'm here.'

'You don't think it has anything to do with your wit and your beauty?'

'Please don't insult me with sarcasm.'

'You don't like compliments?'

'I don't like prevarication, which you seem a master of.'

'I am a master of many things, *cara*.'

'As well as boasting, you mean?'

'Why is it considered a flaw to simply state facts?' He gave the flicker of a smile. 'Very well. Since last night I've been more than a little *puzzled* by your behaviour, Nicola.'

'Oh?'

'Mmm… Usually you come over as one of the most buttoned-up women I've ever met—an attitude which is not without appeal.'

'Appealing to you has never been my intention.'

'And then I run into you,' he said, completely

ignoring her intervention, 'working in a nightclub, looking—'

'Different?' she supplied, using the most innocuous word she could think of.

'You could say that.'

'Maybe I'm just one of those people who likes a little contrast in their life,' she said quickly, because the last thing she wanted him dwelling on was that frivolous little costume. She didn't want to think of that electric-blue gaze skating over her thighs and her bottom, or to imagine him following that visual assessment with the slow drift of his fingers… 'You know,' she added, helpfully, trying to ignore the lump which had risen in her throat. 'Someone who likes a bit of variety.'

The wave of his hand was impatient, as if her arguments had failed to impress him. 'No. It doesn't seem to add up,' he continued, his gaze burning into her like a laser. 'So why are you doing it, Nicola?'

'Isn't it obvious? I need the money.'

'But surely Sergio must pay you a decent wage.'

She wanted to tell him her finances were none of his business, but instinct told her that an alpha man like Alessio di Bari would persist until he got some answers. His curiosity was aroused and he would wish to have it satisfied, because he was a rich and entitled man and that was what men like him were like.

So make the story real, but not too real. Be creative with the truth.

Her mouth twisted into a smile edged with bitterness. Wasn't that the way the world operated? What she'd had to do countless times in the past when social services had come looking for her and her little brother. There was nothing wrong with admitting to problems in your life—you just had to convince the people in power that you could deal with them. 'I'm in debt,' she said baldly.

'Again, a little surprising,' he mused.

'Oh?'

He shrugged. 'That someone who always seems so cool and in control should allow her finances to get out of hand.' His eyes glittered as he circled the tip of his finger round the rim of his wine glass. 'How did that come about?'

'Oh, you know. I overextended myself with my mortgage,' she elaborated, really getting into it now. 'I was a bit too cavalier with the credit card—it's surprisingly easy to spend money you don't have, these days. Before I knew it, I owed the bank a shedload of money.' She paused, unable to keep a note of defiance from her voice. 'Something I don't imagine you've ever been familiar with.'

Alessio nodded as he acknowledged the accusation behind her words, but for some reason her easy assumption irritated him. Was she totally lacking in imagination? Did she think that just because he was a wealthy man, he'd never known hardship, or pain? He wondered how she might react if she knew the real story. But he didn't need to prove himself to her or tell her just how wrong she was. There was only one reason he had invited her here tonight and she had just provided him with the perfect opening.

'How much do you need?' he questioned suddenly.

'I'm sorry?'

'You heard me. Don't look so shocked, Nicola. I said, how much money do you need?'

Her neat blonde hair was gleaming in the candlelight, her grey eyes narrowed with the glint of suspicion. 'What's it got to do with you?'

'Because I could help you.'

'That's the whole point of having a second job! I don't need your help.'

'Are you sure?' He frowned. 'Because unless we're talking six-figure sums—and I imagine you might be in jail if you owed *that* kind of figure— it would be easy for me to give you the money you need. So I'll ask you again. How much?'

He could see her hesitation and the brief flare of silent desperation on her face before she blurted out a sum which was less than he'd spend on a weekend in Paris.

'That's nothing,' he said.

'Maybe to you it isn't—but it's certainly not *nothing* to me!' she declared fiercely.

'I could write off your debt in one fell swoop,' he said. 'In fact, I'd be prepared to double the amount. How does that sound?'

Now her grey eyes were as wide as saucers. 'But why?' she questioned breathlessly. 'I mean, why would you do that?'

He waited while two steaming plates of pasta were deposited on the table in front of them and, although it was his favourite *cacio e pepe*, he paid the food little attention. 'Because I need a favour.'

He saw the veiled look which obliterated the sudden spring of hope in her eyes and made them grow hard.

'What kind of favour?' she questioned woodenly.

The inference behind her question was deeply insulting and Alessio wondered whether working in a club like that had given her a jaundiced view of life. Did she really think he was offering her money to have sex with him? That he was the kind of man who needed to *pay*? His initial response to such a negative character assessment was one of anger, but there was something about the way she'd started biting her lip—a glimpse of unexpected vulnerability lying behind the suspicious mask—which made him soften his stance a little.

'Let me reassure you that what I am proposing is perfectly above-board,' he informed her coolly. 'You need something and I need something. Namely, a woman to accompany me to my mother's sixtieth birthday party next weekend.' He shrugged. 'It's a simple financial transaction, Nicola—nothing more complicated than that.'

'Oh, come on. I'm not completely stupid.' She had relaxed her frozen position but her gaze was still narrowed with suspicion. 'Are you trying to tell me there's nobody else you can ask? Surely you must have a little black book with hundreds of candidates more suitable than me.'

'Indeed I do,' he agreed softly. 'But the trouble with taking a lover on a gig like that is that she'll start to think it's significant.'

'She'll start to think it's significant,' she repeated slowly.

'Introducing her to the family. You know. Take a woman home to meet your mother and before you know it, she'll be trying on long white dresses and organising hen nights.'

'Oh, my goodness. How little you seem to think of my sex,' she breathed. 'Do you really imagine they would be so scheming—or so desperate—to want to be married to a man like you?'

'I hate to disillusion you, Nicola, but yes, they would. But let me be candid with you, and tell you that your fervent words give me a great deal of pleasure.' His voice lowered. 'Since they reassure me you won't be thinking along those lines yourself.'

'Too right I'm not. I'm not interested in marriage.' She pulled a face. 'And even if I *were* looking for a husband it would be someone who was the polar opposite of you!'

'Then why don't you think about my offer instead? You'll get flown out to Umbria—'

'Did...?' There was a brief pause and now she was sitting up very straight in her seat. 'Did you say Umbria?'

'*Sì*, the party is in Italy.'

'I know where Umbria is,' she hissed, before taking a big gulp of water. 'Why take anyone? Why not just go on your own?'

'I've come to the conclusion that wouldn't be the best option,' he said, without missing a beat. He certainly wasn't going to explain that, with a third party present, his poisonous stepfather and two half-siblings might be less inclined to stir up mischief and malcontent. That their company would *possibly* be more tolerable if it was diluted by another person. He wanted Nicola Bennett to agree to his proposal, not send her screaming in the opposite direction. 'All you need to do is to be polite and charming for a few days. I'm sure even you could manage that.'

She raised her eyebrows. 'Surely that would depend on how much time I'm expected to spend with you!'

'And since my mother is a stickler for convention,' he murmured, biting back a reluctant smile, 'we won't even have to be in the same room.'

'I should hope not!' she said, her voice rising with

what sounded like genuine horror, which Alessio also found deeply offensive.

'And for undertaking a simple task in one of the most beautiful regions of Italy, you get to write off your outstanding debts and have enough left to provide you with a cushion,' he continued, his voice dipping as he slipped into the familiar role of negotiation. 'Think about that, Nicola. No more having to work past midnight in some questionable nightclub. No more worrying that someone is going to rumble you to Sergio.'

His gaze dropped to her outfit. It was a perfectly respectable dress the colour of vanilla ice cream, but that was about all you could say about it. She obviously hadn't decided to go shopping after work after all, he decided wryly. Just as she hadn't loosened her glorious hair so that he could feast his eyes on it again, but had tied it into its usual forbidding pleat. He realised he'd only ever seen her at opposite ends of the sartorial spectrum—repressed or tarty—neither of which would work for the forthcoming weekend. And wasn't the truth that he was curious to see what she looked like in something pretty? 'You'll need some suitable clothes to wear, of course, and I'm perfectly happy to foot the bill.'

Her grey eyes narrowed. 'You don't think my existing wardrobe will work?'

'No.'

'Do you…?' She seemed to steady her breathing. 'Do get off on being so insulting?'

'But you asked me a straightforward question, Nicola. I'm a scientist. I deal with facts. Would you prefer me to lie to you?'

'No. But I certainly think you could benefit from a crash course in diplomacy.'

Alessio studied her, aware that some of the layers surrounding her were being peeled away tonight, and that behind that glacial exterior seemed to beat the heart of a tempestuous woman. Was that really so? Unprepared for the sudden sweet ambush of desire, he leaned back in his chair. 'So what do you say?' he questioned unsteadily. 'Are you tempted?'

She shook her head. 'Not in the least.'

'Are you sure?' he persisted, recognising that her refusal was spurring him on, because how long since he'd had to fight for a woman? Fight for anything? 'You wouldn't have to strut around wearing that abbreviated feathery nonsense any more.'

'For all you know, I might enjoy dressing up like that.'

'But you don't,' he said suddenly, with a certainty which came from deep inside him, though he wasn't sure where. 'You don't enjoy men looking at you with hunger in their eyes and talking to your breasts, do you? In fact, I suspect that the prim Nicola Bennett I see at the gallery is a far more accurate reflection of your true character than the blonde showstopper in the skimpy outfit, swaying in her high heels.' He paused. 'Am I right?'

Nicola hesitated. Yes, damn him, he was totally right. But she didn't want him to be. She didn't want his perception or his understanding. She wanted him to vanish into thin air and take his ridiculously attractive offer with him.

But his words were buzzing around inside her head like a mosquito in a cheap hotel bedroom and she couldn't seem to keep her unwelcome thoughts at bay.

She thought about Callum and the mess he'd made of his life. How it hurt like hell to imagine her baby brother in a prison cell.

She thought about his girlfriend, Stacey, and the helpless little infant who would soon depend on her.

On all of them.

Soon she was going to have to help Stacey learn how to be a mother—and how could she possibly do that if she was working nights at the Masquerade club, with the inevitable lack of sleep which came with the job? The rocky road ahead was fraught with enough potholes already, but surely Alessio's offer was giving her the opportunity to smooth it out.

The waiter had reappeared and was looking questioningly at the untouched bowls of pasta in front of them, which smelt absolutely wonderful, though Nicola didn't recognise the dish.

'*Cacio e pepe*—pasta with cheese and pepper,'

Alessio informed her, his blue eyes shadowed by the shuttering of his dark lashes. 'And I'd like your answer before we eat. Unfinished business spoils the meal, I always find.'

The delicious aroma wafted towards her, adding to the general overloading of her senses, and it took a serious effort for Nicola to get her head around this opportunity, which was hers for the taking. Alessio was prepared to give her double what she needed and all she had to do was spend a few days in Italy with him and his family.

Double.

How hard could it be?

But nothing was ever straightforward. If something sounded too good to be true, it was usually because it was. And still she wasn't confronting the most complicating factor of all. Her feelings for Signor di Bari. Or rather, her *sexual* feelings, which, no matter how much she wanted to, she couldn't deny.

She had spent her whole life terrified of intimacy because she had seen what the fallout could be—and her determination not to make the mistakes of her feckless mother had led to her keeping herself to herself. It was a habit so deeply engrained that she didn't even have to think about it. Her lack of engagement with the opposite sex came as easily as breathing—though up until now it had never been tested. And then along had come Alessio di Bari and blown all her preconceived ideas out of the water. He had set her blood on fire right from the get-go. Didn't that add an extra layer of danger to his proposal? Wouldn't increased proximity to his particular brand of arrogant charm only make her more susceptible to him?

Nicola's fingers tightened around her napkin. If it was just her, she would refuse—but it wasn't just her, was it? Could she honestly turn him down?

'Very well. I'll do it,' she said at last.

'*Madonna mia...* I don't think I've ever had to wait so long for an answer.'

She frowned. 'And we'll definitely be getting separate rooms?'

'Count on it, *cara*. Believe me, the thought of waking up to your disapproving expression doesn't fill me with any joy.' He picked up his fork. 'You need to be ready to leave on Friday.'

'And presumably you don't want me to mention anything about this to Sergio?'

'Probably better not to.' He glittered her a complicit smile. 'It might complicate matters if he knew we were spending the weekend together.'

'We're not spending the weekend *together*,' she corrected repressively. 'It's just a couple of days we need to get through as best we can.'

She saw him bite back a smile and wished he hadn't, because it made his features relax and she wondered if he was aware just how blindingly beautiful he looked in that moment.

'How severely you dent my ego, Nicola,' he murmured.

'If anyone's ego can take a little denting, it has to be yours.' Dragging her gaze away from him, she focussed instead on her plate of pasta. After sealing such an uneasy deal, some women might have been keen to get away, or have lost their appetite, but not Nicola. When you'd known real hunger, it always seemed like a sin to turn down a good meal.

Bending her head, she began to eat.

CHAPTER FOUR

As the house came into view Alessio slowed the car, feeling an inevitable tension begin to creep into his body. His reaction to these surroundings was predictable despite his having stayed away for years, yet nobody could deny the beauty of the place. He gave a bitter smile. Least of all him.

With Nicola beside him, he had driven past tiny terracotta-roofed houses, clinging to the edges of dark green hills. His powerful car had passed through sleepy village squares, where locals drank tiny cups of coffee and exquisite churches rang out the Angelus. There were fields of cows the colour of caramel, and other fields splashed yellow by sunflowers or bright, scarlet poppies. Up here in the hills, it was more remote. His stepfather's estate was surrounded by forests in which wild boar roamed free and the sunsets over the distant lake were among the most beautiful he had ever seen. Yet Alessio wished he were anywhere else in the world than here.

But wishes rarely came true—that had been a lesson he'd learnt early on. In approximately fifteen minutes' time he would be driving through the electronic gates of his stepfather's enormous mansion, ready to face the inevitable family disharmony. He wondered why the hell he hadn't just bought his mother an extravagant present and taken her out to lunch next time he was in London, or in Paris.

Because she would never have forgiven you.

Because, despite her many flaws, she's still your mother.

And didn't he sometimes despise that biological connection which could draw you back to the bitterness of the past?

'Okay. So what do I need to know before we get there?' asked Nicola, her crisp words breaking into his uncomfortable reverie. 'You haven't really said.'

He turned to look at her. He had been so deep in thought during the journey that at times he had almost forgotten she was there. He swept her an assessing look, silently applauding his insistence she acquire the services of a personal shopper, because the Nicola Bennett who was outlined against the green and gold of the Tuscan countryside looked like a completely different woman. Her summer dress caressed the high curve of her breasts and the floaty skirt outlined her slender thighs in a way which was...

He swallowed. *Compelling.* There was no other

word for it. Her hair was piled on top of her head in its usual helmet style, but it showcased her long and swan-like neck. Suddenly Alessio found himself imagining how it would feel to have her in his arms and the taste of her soft lips beneath his. Suddenly he wanted to trail his tongue over that soft flesh, only this time to find the rose-shaped birthmark above her breasts and explore it. He wanted to strip her bare and lose himself in the hidden and forbidden areas of her body and he wanted all these things with an urgency which took his breath away.

Yet she had done nothing to this incite the potent stir of desire which was heating his blood. She hadn't flirted, or chatted. In fact, she had been almost completely silent during the journey, which had pleased him—though conversely it had also irritated him that he wasn't having to bat off the predictable remarks women often made when you put them in a powerful car and drove through some very expensive real estate. He frowned. Even on entering his private jet, she had failed to make the usual calculating murmurs which always served to reinforce his many prejudices about her sex.

'What do you want to know?' he questioned silkily.

'Who's going to be there, for a start.'

'My mother, obviously. And my stepfather.'

'Okay. So did…?' She pushed her sunglasses further up her nose. 'You haven't really talked about them. Did your parents get divorced, or did your father die?'

Impatiently, he pulled over and killed the engine, tapping his fingers against the steering wheel. 'Why on earth is that relevant?'

'Because I'm going to be a guest in their home,' she said. 'I'm just operating on a need-to-know basis, that's all—I'm not interested in anything else. And it's useful to discover some of the background behind their relationship, should the subject come up.'

'I can assure you that there won't be any discussion about their relationship,' he said, with a short, cynical laugh. 'My stepfather's name is Edward Bonner. Lord Bonner,' he elaborated, because the man had always been a crashing snob and woe betide Nicola Bennett if she had the temerity to call him *mister*.

'You mean he's…he's a member of the aristocracy?'

He heard the note of apprehension which had entered her voice.

'I'm afraid so.'

'And he's English?'

'Yes. He's been married to my Italian mother for nearly thirty years.'

'Wow.' Some of her caution evaporated. 'That's… well, that's wonderful.'

'In what way is it "wonderful"?' he questioned sarcastically.

'To have such a long marriage. Especially second

time around. You know the stats for *those*. Doom and gloom.' She hesitated. 'They must be very happy.'

His eyebrows shot up. 'Since you know nothing about the background, isn't that a somewhat naïve assumption to make—especially coming from a woman who says she isn't interested in marriage?'

'Just because marriage doesn't appeal to me personally, doesn't mean I can't appreciate one which has overcome the odds!'

Alessio didn't enlighten her. Why be the one to destroy her ideals? Let her discover for herself just where his family featured on the happiness register. He gave a bitter smile. Wasn't that what he was paying her for? To tolerate a weekend of dysfunction and make it more bearable. 'My younger half-brother and half-sister, Sebastian and Lydia, will be there. There'll be a quiet family dinner tonight and a big party tomorrow.' He started the engine again. 'Anything else you want to know?'

Yes, there was plenty, but his tone sounded so forbidding that Nicola shook her head as the car pulled away. What a difficult man he was turning out to be, she thought, tearing her gaze away from his wind-ruffled hair. Increased exposure certainly hadn't altered her negative opinion of him.

He'd barely said a word on the flight over, just buried himself in a heap of work—and she had taken the hint and kept quiet. He'd even taken a phone call from a woman and agreed that he'd take her out for dinner next time he was in Munich, which for some reason Nicola had found intensely irritating. Plus, he hadn't even remarked on her new clothes or changed appearance, which was oddly hurtful as he'd been so critical of it before. Especially as she had reluctantly accepted the ministrations of the personal shopper he had arranged to take her in hand.

Against the backdrop of one of London's glitziest department stores, it had been a surreal experience to realise that as many new clothes as she needed for the weekend were to be hers, with money no option. Imagine that. Nicola had blinked in disbelief at one of the price tags, while the stylist had been rifling through the rails. She'd seen these kinds of clothes on the women who came into the gallery but wearing them herself was a completely new experience. She wondered what it must feel like to have unlimited wealth at your disposal. Did you become blasé if you never had to think about the cost, and would that explain some of Alessio's cynicism?

Yet despite her inner pep talks, she could feel her palms growing clammy as the powerful car whipped through the stunning Tuscan countryside and she thought about what lay ahead. Alessio's stepfather was a lord, which was a pretty big deal to someone from her background, and he was English. Did that explain Alessio's unique accent—the slightly crystal inflection which underpinned his sexy Italian drawl and made him so hard to pin down?

Nicola had done a lot of work on her own way of speaking and had smoothed out the worst of her early accent. But what if his family saw through her and realised the kind of person she really was? Suddenly, she was nervous. Because, yes, she was employed by a successful man and no stranger to the trappings of wealth—but those things had always been at a distance removed. Maintaining an air of confidence at an art show after-party with her influential boss was very different from spending a whole weekend under the microscope as a bogus date, with people who were of a completely different class to her. What if she let Alessio—or herself—down? What if she committed some terrible cringe-making gaffe, like the time she'd almost drunk the bowl of lemon water after eating shellfish, instead of dipping her fingers into it? Would that mean he wouldn't pay her?

Nicola's heart raced.

He *had* to pay her.

Because she had gone round to Stacey's bedsit last night, her stomach sinking as she'd registered the dirty dishes cluttering up the sink and general air of neglect. She had opened up the empty fridge, slotting in the cartons of soft fruit, olives and hummus she'd brought with her—which would hopefully tempt the pregnant woman into eating more than the biscuits which had been the only food on show.

It had taken an effort but Nicola had injected a note of forced jollity into her voice as she'd surveyed the sullen profile of her brother's girlfriend. 'I'm going to have a surprise for you after the weekend, Stacey,' she announced.

But Stacey had barely stirred from her rapt preoccupation with a TV programme about a family who seemed to be inexplicably cutting all ties with their English life to go and live in remote Spain. 'What sort of surprise?'

'Ah!' Nicola had waggled her finger in the manner of a cartoon fairy godmother. 'If I tell you now, it won't be a surprise, will it?'

For once, Stacey had turned away from the screen, a flicker of interest shining briefly in her eyes. 'Okay. I'm cool with that.'

And that was the trouble with money, Nicola decided. It had a power all of its own. It could change the way you felt and the way you reacted. Now she'd envisaged getting the life-changing amount Alessio had promised her she couldn't countenance *not* getting it. The thought of going back to the Masquerade club and dealing with all those leering punters filled her with dread.

But that wasn't going to happen.

She was a fighter, not a quitter. She was going to make this weekend work, no matter what they—or he—threw at her.

'We're here,' Alessio drawled as the car slowed in front of a giant set of wrought-iron gates and Nicola stared ahead. As the gates opened she saw a long path, which led to an enormous cream mansion. Manicured lawns were dotted with bronze statues which glinted in the afternoon sun, and there were flowerbeds bright with roses and daisies. In the distance she could see a walkway edged with the purple haze of lavender and imagined all the bees buzzing contentedly there. But it was the house itself which dominated everything. Flanked by the dark spears of cypress trees, it was tall and statuesque, its soaring marble columns only adding to its majestic beauty.

'Oh,' she said, a little breathlessly.

He shot her a glance. 'Like it?'

On one level, yes, of course she did, for who could fail to like such a magnificent pile? But she found herself thinking it looked more like a palace than a home. 'It's very impressive.'

'I think that's the whole point,' he said drily.

As the car drew closer Nicola could see an older woman standing in the porticoed doorway, her black dress chic and her hair neatly styled. 'Is that your mother?' she questioned nervously.

'Actually, it's my stepfather's French housekeeper, Genevieve.'

Inside, something in Nicola died. Gaffe number one. Tick. 'I'm so sorry. I thought—'

'Don't worry about it.' He switched off the engine and passed the car keys through the open window to a young valet who had appeared from the back of the property. 'It's an easy mistake to make. Who could blame you for thinking that the welcoming committee might actually be a member of my family? No doubt my mother will be inside.' His lips curved. 'With her husband.'

Did Nicola imagine the scorn in his voice? She thought about her own mother, who had a catalogue of defects as long as your arm. But Nicola couldn't imagine her not running out to greet her in person. What *had* she let herself in for? she wondered as the housekeeper inclined her head deferentially towards Alessio, before shaking Nicola by the hand.

'Your mother has asked would you please wait in the south sitting room,' said Genevieve, in her soft French accent. 'She and Lord Bonner will be with you shortly.'

They followed the housekeeper up the short flight of steps into the house and an entrance hall of breathtaking dimensions, where the air was thick with the scent of lilies. But Nicola didn't get the chance to study any of the priceless artworks which would have usually made her drool, because they were being led into a vast sitting room.

She glanced around the room, taking in the enormous marble fireplace, the floor-to-ceiling nineteenth-century portraits, and several sets of French windows, which overlooked a stunning garden. At Genevieve's suggestion, Nicola perched nervously on the edge of a velvet chair, but Alessio was pacing the room like a caged lion. As the minutes ticked by it became impossible to ignore the increasingly stony set of his features and implacable line of his unsmiling mouth, and although conversation was the last thing she wanted to engage in, she couldn't hold back the question any longer.

'Is everything…okay?'

Electric-blue eyes narrowed. 'I'm not sure I understand what you're asking.'

Why was he doing that remote thing, which made her feel so inadequate? 'I'm just not sure why we're being made to wait like this. I mean…surely your mother must be anxious to see you? I'm sorry,' she amended quickly when she saw his face darken. 'It's probably none of my business.'

'You're right, it's not,' he snapped, then seemed to relent. 'Don't worry about it, Nicola. It's a power thing.'

But before she could ask any more—which he obviously didn't want her to—they were disturbed by the arrival of the couple and Nicola scrambled to her feet, a little unsteady in the new pink espadrilles which matched her dress. Introductions were made and her first impression was that Alessio's mother, Rosetta, must have been an absolute stunner in her time because she was still a startlingly beautiful woman. She was petite and slim, her dark hair was threaded with silver and her bone structure was amazing. It was easy to see where Alessio had got his looks from, Nicola thought, even though his eyes were blue, not brown. But she thought the greeting between mother and son was decidedly subdued. From the lack of warmth in their embrace, they might have been casual acquaintances meeting at a cocktail party.

Rosetta's husband, Edward, was at least twenty years older than his wife, his upright stance suggesting a career in the military. But his faded grey eyes were calculating as they looked Nicola up and down and she wondered if he could see right through her. Did he realise that she'd been born in one of the roughest parts of London and that her early years had been total chaos? That she was the last person who Alessio would *genuinely* have dated?

'Please. Sit down. Let's have some refreshment.' Lord Bonner waved his hand and, as if it had been timed to the second—which it probably had—Genevieve appeared with a young maid, bringing in all the accoutrements for afternoon tea, which they proceeded to lay out on a beautifully polished mahogany table.

It felt strange to be offered scones and cake in the centre of Italy, but Nicola accepted only a cup of milkless tea, terrified of ladling cream and jam on the scone in the wrong order, which people seemed to get really exercised about in certain parts of England. She sat back while Alessio and his mother chatted about the family dinner that night, which would be followed by the bigger birthday party the following evening—all beneath the oddly unsettling and watchful stare of Lord Bonner. Nicola wondered if she was imagining the inexplicable undercurrents which were making the atmosphere around the small table feel so tense.

'So...' Rosetta plucked at her linen napkin nervously. 'Have you and my son been together very long, Nicola?'

Momentarily, Nicola froze.

Why on earth hadn't they rehearsed the answer to this?

She wondered what they would say if she told them the truth.

No, I try to keep out of his way as much as possible because I find him arrogant and unbearable and he does dangerous things to my heart-rate.

Or, even worse...

Actually, he's paying me to be here.

But her hesitation was due to more than her conflicting feelings. She simply didn't know how a woman in a loving relationship was supposed to respond to a question like that, because she'd never been in one before. The smile she directed at Alessio was uncertain. 'We've—'

'Known each other for quite a while, haven't we, Nicky?' Alessio glittered her a look which suggested she needed to up her game. 'What you might call a *slow burn...*'

Slow burn was about right—that was if the sudden rise of heat in her usually cool cheeks was anything to go by. 'That's right. We…erm…we met in London.' Nicola licked her lips. 'My boss has an art gallery and Alessio is one of his best friends, as well as one of our best customers.'

'But no purchase has ever seemed quite so valuable as you are to me, *tesoro mio*,' said Alessio smoothly, and he leant across the table and briefly squeezed her hand.

Nicola stiffened and not just because his unexpected touch had made her breasts and her tummy tighten. It was more to do with the sudden gleam which had entered Lord Bonner's eyes— as if he recognised that the gesture was meaningless. And suddenly she realised that he didn't like his stepson one bit.

'Ah, young love,' the baron said reflectively, giving a theatrical sigh. 'Always such a delight to witness. Thank heavens I've managed to talk your mother out of some of her more old-fashioned ideas, Alessio. I keep telling her she needs to move with the times. So we've put you both in the lake room. I think you'll be very comfortable in there.'

'Perfetto,' Alessio murmured, rising gracefully to his feet and holding out his hand to Nicola, and she was so discombobulated by what she'd heard that she took it, resenting the warm caress of his fingers, while somehow revelling in it at the same time. 'I think we might go and freshen up.' He turned to his

mother. 'Mamma, perhaps we should have a few moments on our own before dinner? Is that something which is going to be possible?'

Nicola was aware of how nervous Rosetta seemed in response to her son's suggestion. Her beautiful dark eyes were clouded with apprehension and her expression was fretful as she looked at her husband, as if she wanted to say something but didn't dare.

'I'm sure that can be arranged,' said Lord Bonner smoothly.

After thanking their hosts, Alessio led her away, still holding her hand—with the older couple watching them in tense silence. They exited the grand sitting room to ascend a sweeping staircase to the first floor, but she didn't trust herself to say a single word until the door swung closed behind them and she found herself alone with the Italian billionaire.

Alone in an enormous bedroom, with an equally enormous bed.

And although her mind was buzzing with questions about why his mother seemed so jumpy and his stepfather so scary, there was really only one thing on her mind.

CHAPTER FIVE

'THIS IS…*INTOLERABLE*!' Nicola declared, snatching her hand away from his.

Rather missing the rapid slam of her pulse beneath his fingers, Alessio watched as she plucked her sunglasses from the top of her head and hurled them onto the four-poster bed, where they sank into the luxurious brocade. He'd never seen Miss Cool lose her temper before. Never even imagined she was capable of it. It was like seeing a stone statue suddenly become flesh and he found he couldn't tear his eyes away from her tempestuous beauty.

'What's wrong?' he murmured, noting that a strand of blonde hair had broken free from its confinement. *At last.* It was the first crack he had seen in her armour and yet the subsequent kick of lust which powered through his veins bemused him. He had witnessed her in a nightclub with little more than a flurry of feathers adorning her delicious bottom and her long legs encased in a pair of fishnet stockings—

so why the hell did a fallen strand of hair suddenly seem so intensely erotic?

'You know exactly what's wrong, Signor di Bari—so please don't give me that wide-eyed look of bewilderment! I could just about forgive the episode of hand-holding downstairs, which I *suppose* was necessary to make our relationship seem more convincing, but not this. Definitely not this.' She glared at him. 'You promised me separate rooms. You promised! That was the only reason I agreed to come.'

'The only reason?' he echoed coolly. 'Are you sure about that? You don't think your big fat pay cheque might have something to do with it?'

'You said we wouldn't have to share! You told me your mother was old-fashioned about that kind of thing.' She looked at the enormous bed and then quickly turned away from it. 'I definitely didn't sign up for this!'

'And neither did I,' he said, thinking that her shudder might have been amusing, if it hadn't also been the strangest kind of *turn-on*. 'This wasn't supposed to happen.'

'Then why,' she said, 'has it?'

There was silence as Alessio felt his body tense, resenting the ability of the past to impact on the present. No wonder he had stayed away so long. No wonder his heart sank whenever he strayed into the poisonous atmosphere which surrounded his family.

He thought how best to convey the facts, because, as Nicola herself had said, this was purely on a need-to-know basis. And he wanted her to know as little as possible. About him. About his life. Because knowledge was all about power and, ultimately, control and he was reluctant to relinquish either of those things.

'I suspect my stepfather is playing games and doing something designed to cause mischief. It's a particular talent of his,' he added acidly. 'My mother doesn't approve of her unmarried children sharing rooms with members of the opposite sex, and everyone has always gone along with her wishes.'

'Seems a little old-fashioned,' she offered cautiously.

'You could say that.' His mouth hardened. 'It's never really bothered me, because I've never brought a woman here.'

'Until now,' she said slowly.

'Until now,' he agreed slowly. 'In fact, this is the first time I've been here for years.'

'So what made you change your mind about coming?'

Alessio turned away from the hypnotic beauty of her grey eyes and walked over to the window, where the formal grounds outside the house contrasted incongruously with the wild forest beyond. But the stunning setting was lost on him—because how could you possibly appreciate beauty in such a hostile environment? He hadn't intended to tell her anything about his family dynamic, but now he recognised he couldn't keep her totally in the dark. She was an intelligent woman and if he wanted her cooperation, she would require some kind of explanation. Because wasn't he buying her compliance, as well as her company?

He turned back to face her, momentarily startled by how changed she appeared in the intimate setting of the bedroom. The errant strand of hair was still dangling around her flushed cheek, and he got a sudden idea of how she might look first thing in the morning. All creamy flesh and pale blonde hair spread across the pillow. Her curvy body soft beneath the sheet. His throat tightened. How the hell was he going to resist her when she was looking at him like that?

Across the vast expanse of the room their gazes locked, her eyes growing dark, and he heard the catch of breath in her throat, as if acknowledging the sudden pulse of attraction which was throbbing through the air between them. But he shook his head, closing his mind to the automatic parting of her lips, which were making him want to kiss her, and steeling his sudden desire as best he could. There were a million reasons why having sex with Nicola Bennett was a bad idea, and having to share a bedroom was adding an unbearable layer of temptation. But it would do him good to resist her. It was something he'd never had to do before— and wasn't he always keen to embrace the novel whenever it came his way?

'What's different is that it's my mother's mile-stone birthday, which means I needed to make an effort—and this is precisely why you are here, Nicola. To defuse the atmosphere. To give everyone something else to think about, other than the usual petty squabbling over their inheritance.' He paused, a wry smile touching the edges of his lips. 'But given my reputation as something of a commitment-phobe, you should be prepared for some fairly insolent questions about how serious our relationship is.' He raised his eyebrows. 'It might add a little more conviction if you could try not to recoil whenever I come near you.'

'I'll try.' She huffed out a sigh. 'But believe me, this is the last thing I wanted.'

'Ditto, *cara*. I'm not exactly jumping for joy myself.'

And wasn't that just typical of a woman? he thought. The moment he mentioned that he *didn't* want to be alone with her—she extended her bottom lip in a brief but unmistakable pout. Was she offended by his assertion that he didn't want to be alone with her? Did she *want* him to acknowledge the desire which was simmering between them, or pretend it didn't exist?

'Don't worry. Nothing's going to happen. We can put a line of cushions down the centre of the bed as a temporary barricade,' he suggested drily. 'If that'll make you feel better.'

'The only thing which will make me feel better is when I'm on that plane going back to England.'

He could see her gritting her teeth behind her lips and he felt another flicker of disbelief. Didn't she realise how many women would have moved heaven and earth to find themselves alone with him like this? Women who, by now, would have been showering him with hungry kisses and unzipping his fly.

'In the interests of authenticity let's at least try to be civil to each another, shall we?' he snapped. 'I'm going to take a shower.'

'Take your time.'

'Oh, don't worry, I will.'

After he'd gone into the bathroom, Nicola resisted the temptation to drag her hairbrush from her handbag and hurl it at the door which he'd slammed shut behind him. But instead, she sucked in a few deep breaths, in a futile attempt to calm herself. What was the *matter* with her? Was she, someone who was always so calm and collected, actually contemplating *throwing a hairbrush*? Why was she letting Alessio di Bari get underneath her skin like this?

She knew why. It was because she wanted him. The truth was that she had always wanted him and being trapped like this meant it was getting increasingly difficult to hide that fact. Over the years she had deliberately put a stopper on her feelings, not wanting messy emotions to hijack the strange double life she had forged for herself. It had never been a problem because nobody had ever captured her imagination or her emotions before. But emotion was what was rushing over her now and it was powerful and all-consuming. She could hear the sound of gushing water from the other side of the bathroom door and the thought of Alessio standing naked beneath the shower was enough to send her senses into overdrive.

She imagined his bare chest.

Bare arms.

Bare bottom.

Imagined water cascading over all that darkly golden flesh. A tug of heat clenched low in her sex and suddenly she felt so weak she was no longer certain her feet would support her. Sitting down on the edge of the bed, she untied her espadrilles and slumped back on the mattress, her heart racing. She stared up at the enormous chandelier which was dangling from the ceiling, like a cascade of diamonds suspended in mid-air.

How was she going to tolerate an entire weekend if this was what it was going to be like? Because no matter how enormous the room—and it *was* enormous—there was still only one bed. How was she going to pretend she couldn't care less about him? She wasn't *that* good an actress. Even worse, she didn't actually know the protocol for sharing a room with a man, because she'd never done it before. Would he laugh if he knew the truth? Of course he would. She was a modern-day freak, which was why she always kept it quiet.

Actually, I've reached the grand old age of twenty-five and I'm still a virgin. She imagined the coolly questioning look she would direct at him before remarking, *I know. It is unusual, isn't it?*

Nicola had spent her whole life learning the kind of things which most people took for granted. She'd learnt how to read and write long after most girls her age. How to hold a knife and fork properly and iron out the harsh way of speaking which she'd picked up during her first few feral years. She had been a diligent student and largely successful in most things she had turned her hand to. She had studied on buses, on Tubes or whenever she got the chance. While her peers had been buying lipsticks and giggling about boys, she'd always had her head in a book. When she'd got the opportunity to work in the high-octane art world, she had diligently watched how other people behaved and successfully copied them. But inside she could feel like that little girl who sensed the whole world was against her.

But this was different. This wasn't something you could *learn*. You couldn't watch other women and mimic their actions when they were alone with a man. Because—unless they were engaged in one of those *ménage à trois* situations you sometimes read about—bedroom etiquette wasn't actually a spectator sport.

So how *did* you go about cohabiting with a man you weren't in a relationship with? She bit her lip. She supposed she would have to get undressed in the bathroom. Would he let her go first—or should she defer to him, since he was paying her? She was definitely going to wear the baggy T-shirt she'd brought from home—not the slippery and highly revealing nightgown, which the personal shopper had insisted she purchase.

Her eyes flickered towards the heavy antique furniture and the big vases of blousy roses which were dotted everywhere, their petals spilling onto the polished wood. She was feeling uncomfortably warm, so she undid a button on her dress, but that did little to cool her heated skin. Her thoughts were spinning so fast that Nicola shut her eyes in an attempt to block out some of the visual stimuli which were playing havoc with her senses. But the perfume of the roses was powerful and the warm Umbrian air which filtered in through the open windows felt deliciously soft on her bare arms.

She could feel her eyelids growing heavy and her limbs were growing heavy, too—as if someone had coated them in liquid gold and weighted them down to the bed. Suddenly, she realised she'd hardly slept a wink in the preceding days because she'd been so worried about Stacey and Callum, and also, of course, about this trip. But now all her worries were being dominated by her body's need for rest. They were seeping away, like raindrops on leaves, evaporating in the sunshine. For a while she drifted away on a fragrant cloud, until a sound started beckoning her reluctantly back down to earth.

It was a voice, she thought.

A gorgeous voice.

Silk and velvet. Crystal and gravel. And rich, like chocolate.

'Nicola.'

Nobody had ever said her name that way before. *Nee*-co-la. Caressing the three syllables and making it sound incredibly *sexy*. Was that air from the open window fanning her face, or was it something else? Instinct told her it was breath and so did the impression of someone bending over her. How did you realise someone was so close, when your eyes were closed and they weren't even touching you? Her lips seemed to be parting of their own accord and although afterwards she tried to tell herself she didn't know what she was doing, Nicola knew exactly what she was doing. Her hands were reaching up to encounter Alessio's shoulders and she gave a soft sigh of satisfaction as they made contact with the silk shirt covering his flesh. Because wasn't this what she had wanted all along?

For a moment she kneaded the silk-coated muscle, before letting her fingertips drift to his face. With the edge of her thumb she traced the curve of his jaw before allowing it to drift to his upper lip. She heard him utter something indistinct as she outlined the sensual curve and then her heart almost leapt out of her chest because suddenly his mouth was on hers and he was kissing her.

Hungrily.

Frantically.

And she was kissing him back. Her mouth was opening wider to allow his tongue to move inside and Nicola felt as if she had been touched by flame. As if a million stars had exploded. Liquid heat flooded her sex as he deepened the kiss and she moaned with a sense of disbelief. Because although she had been kissed by men before, nothing could have prepared her for *this*. This didn't feel like a clumsy intrusion— this felt like heaven. She could feel the warm drench of desire. The painful prickling of her breasts. The sweet longing pulsing through her body was so insistent that she began to writhe her hips in silent invitation.

Take me, she thought desperately. *Do what you want with me*. And just in case he hadn't got the message, she pressed her breasts against his chest and gave a little moan. And he responded. Pushing her back against the mattress, his hand moved to the front of her dress—undoing several of the buttons before slipping inside to her lacy bra. He didn't even touch her bare skin. His thumb just brushed over her peaking nipple through the lace and Nicola nearly passed out.

It felt unbelievable.

Incredible.

His other hand was on her knee, tiptoeing towards her thigh. Against his lips, Nicola held her breath as an unfamiliar pulse began to beat and, instinctively, she tilted her hips, imploring him to go further. To touch her where she most needed to be touched.

But just as suddenly as it had started, it ended. He pulled away and the absence of his lips and his body felt shocking, as if she had been deprived of something essential, and she made a small sound of protest.

'Open your eyes,' he said roughly.

But Nicola didn't want to. She wanted to keep them shut and carry on with what they were doing. She wanted to forget it was him and just enjoy the way he was making her feel.

'Open your eyes,' he said again, his voice even harsher.

What else could she do but obey that fierce command? Her lashes fluttered open to see his slashed features swimming in and out of focus. He must have been leaning over to wake her up when she had grabbed him, as if he were a lifeline. But he was clearly as affected as her by what had just happened. The pupils of his eyes were dilated, their wild blackness almost obscuring the bright blue.

'I'm perfectly happy to carry on with what we're doing, Nicola,' he said, once he had steadied his breathing. 'But I would prefer some kind of acknowledgement that it's me who is making love to you.' His eyes glittered—hard and bright. 'I would hate to think you're lying there fantasising about someone else. Particularly when you still haven't even said my name.'

And in a way Nicola was grateful for his words, because they killed her desire stone-dead. She swallowed. Well…maybe not *completely* dead—but enough to allow common sense to replace the debilitating sense of longing which kept her anchored to the bed. She wished she had the energy to get up, but she didn't. All she could do was lie there, heavy with heat and hunger as she tried to ignore the crazy pounding of her heart.

His words had made her angry, but his perception made her angrier still. No way had she been fantasising about anyone else—as if anyone else would ever get a look-in while Alessio di Bari had his tongue inside your mouth—but she *had* been just letting it happen and hoping her lack of engagement would absolve her of responsibility for what she was doing.

Yet guilt and fear were powerful motivators and those were what sparked her response to him. 'Wait a minute. I don't think we should be doing this,' she managed, her breath leaving her mouth in infuriatingly short little bursts, while the tingling sensation in her breasts was almost unbearable.

Straightening up, he raked his fingers back through his damp hair, his lips twisting with disdain. 'All I did was try to wake you. As I recall, you were the one who eased me down towards your delicious lips and then lay there, just begging to be taken.'

His raw words were like a bucket of cold water to her senses. Nicola watched as he walked awkwardly towards the window as if something was obstructing his movement and a sudden rush of anxiety washed over her as she thought about what he'd said. Had she really made a pass at him? Grabbed him and forced him to kiss her? Oh, God.

'I didn't mean—'

'Relax, Nicola, I'm just trying to take some of the heat out of the situation' he said, his voice tinged with mockery as he turned to look at her. 'It was just one of those things, that's all.'

She nodded. He made it sound inevitable. Did women always want to have sex with him? As she stared at his powerful body silhouetted against the lush green countryside outside the sharp tightening of her nipples gave her the answer. Of course they did.

'It was?' she managed huskily.

'Of course. Or maybe it was my own fantasy, not yours,' he conceded, his blue eyes glinting with a spark of unholy humour. 'Waking sleeping beauty with a kiss.'

Nobody had ever called her beautiful before, nor described her lips as 'delicious', and Nicola was unsure whether to believe what he was saying. Probably safer not to. People paid you compliments when they wanted something, didn't they? And there was nothing she wanted—or dared—to give him.

So don't just lie there like a passive wuss. *Do* something.

Her prone position putting her at a distinct disadvantage, she rose from the bed with as much dignity as she could muster, smoothing down the crumpled skirt of her dress and tucking an errant strand of hair behind her ear. 'I don't know what came over me,' she said.

'Oh, I think you do,' he offered drily. 'Unexpected proximity coupled with a very powerful sexual chemistry. It's a potent mix and don't pretend you don't know *that*, Nicola. What we do about it, of course,' he added, after a moment's pause, 'is an entirely different matter.'

She stared at him blankly, as the meaning of his words sank in. Was he implying that they could have sex when they weren't even in a relationship? Didn't he realise he was dealing with the biggest prude in London? 'We do nothing, of course,' she informed him primly. And then, because his expression remained perplexed, she took pains to remind him. 'We have a plan, remember?'

'A plan?' he echoed non-comprehendingly.

'Didn't you say something about putting cushions down the middle of the bed?'

Thoughtfully, his eyes narrowed. 'And you really think that's going to work?'

'Why wouldn't it work?' she challenged. 'If it's what we both want.'

He seemed about to answer but maybe he thought better of it, because he firmed his lips as if he were trying very hard not to laugh and it took a moment before he had composed himself enough to speak. '*Certo, cara*—it will be exactly as you say,' he murmured. 'In which case, I'd better leave you to get settled in. This room is proving a little too...claustrophobic for my liking.'

She wondered if he'd forgotten his promise to show her around the estate before dinner, but maybe that was a good thing. 'As you wish.'

'I'm going downstairs to find my mother.' And then, as if he was determined to reassert his authority, his blue eyes glittered with familiar command. 'Make sure you're ready for cocktails at seven.'

CHAPTER SIX

ALESSIO RETURNED FROM his meeting with his mother, walking into their room with his dark features set and brooding, and Nicola looked up at him with some alarm. Now what? she wondered.

'Is everything okay?' she ventured.

'Everything is fine,' he gritted back repressively, his drawled voice growing mocking as he began to unbutton his shirt. 'I don't know your views on voyeurism, Nicola, but I'm about to get changed, so...'

The thought of him stripping off his clothes was enough to send Nicola scuttling outside into the early evening sunset, where she settled herself on a wicker bench and willed the racing of her heart to subside. But the magnificent landscape didn't really register and neither did the book whose pages remained unturned, despite the glowing reviews on the front cover, no doubt courtesy of the author's friends. She couldn't stop thinking about what had happened between the two of them earlier, and kept wishing she could forget it.

But she couldn't.

Round and round in her head it played—an endless spool of provocation and frustration. Alessio had kissed her and she had responded in a way which had spooked her. Because it had been more than a simple kiss, even she knew that. It had felt as though he had flicked a switch—cracking open the stony darkness inside her and flooding her body with heat and desire. She had melted beneath his touch and prayed for him to carry on.

'Nicola?'

He was walking out onto the terrace to find her and Nicola's breath dried in her throat as she saw him in formal tailoring for the very first time. Hugging the contours of his powerful frame, the suit mirrored the blackness of his hair and against the white shirt his skin glowed like burnished metal. But something about his appearance was different—his golden dark beauty somehow compromised. It was as if a shadow had fallen over him. His eyes were cold, his mouth hard and unsmiling—and an instinctive part of her wanted to ask him what the matter was and then reach out and comfort him. But that wasn't why she was here, she reminded herself grimly—though his next words took her by surprise, even though they were delivered in something of a growl.

'You look…' He paused. 'Good,' he finished abruptly.

'Do I?'

Alessio nodded, the insecurity in her eyes making him realise this wasn't the disingenuous query of a woman who was regularly showered with compliments. But then, who would ever have imagined that Nicola Bennett could look like this? Not him and possibly not her either. High-end fashion suited her and the flower-sprinkled green gown hugged the soft curve of her breasts and hips. She looked like a meadow, he thought with sudden longing. Fresh and beautiful. Her long hair had been transmuted into fiery gold by the sunset behind her and it tumbled down to a surprisingly tiny waist.

Suddenly he wanted to bury his lips in those silken strands and to continue the lovemaking he had so reluctantly terminated. But he closed his mind to the unwanted trajectory of his erotic thoughts because her Cinderella-like transformation was not the purpose behind this visit. She was supposed to be a diversion, not a distraction. So what was happening? How come she was making him feel like…?

He shook his head with self-directed impatience.

Like an untried teenager and an experienced man all at once. That kiss had been heady. She had invoked a powerful and intoxicating hunger which had rolled over him like a heavy wave, until he had called a halt to it. And he had never done that before. Never stopped a session of sex just as it was getting started, not when he had wanted it so much. His tongue slid out to ease the dryness of his lips. Lust and restraint—another potent combination.

'Come on,' he said curtly. 'Let's go.'

She followed him down the sweeping staircase towards the garden, where he could hear the murmur of voices, and out onto the terrace. Only his two siblings were there, surveying their luxurious surroundings with an air of proprietorial satisfaction. The relationship between the three of them had always been non-existent at best and hostile at worst, but Alessio reminded himself that he was here to please his mother.

Yet he frowned as he recalled Rosetta's fretful demeanour during their meeting when, although free from the watchful presence of her husband, she had been unable to relax. He remembered the way her gaze had darted repeatedly towards the door and her refusal to disclose what was troubling her, no matter how gently he had persisted with his questions. But she was an adult, he reminded himself—and he could not help her unless she asked for help.

'Come and meet the others,' he said, touching his fingers to Nicola's arm, dipping his head to speak quietly into her ear. 'This probably won't be the friendliest of encounters, but I'm confident you'll be able to deal with it.'

But Nicola was finding it difficult to subdue her sudden clamour of nerves—despite Alessio's supposedly reassuring words, or the touch of his fingers to her elbow. The seeking gazes of the striking couple who stood drinking champagne in the dying sunlight were making her feel inadequate because they were everything she was not—and that pressed all sorts of buttons.

Both younger than Alessio, the man's upright posture was reminiscent of his aristocratic father, while the woman was tall and rangy with an expensive mane of streaked hair, which complemented her golden dress and diamonds. With their perfectly even tans suggesting a lifetime of leisure, they looked glossy and...well, just *rich*, really, with an air of wealth and privilege which went more than skin-deep. Alessio possessed it, too—but she didn't. No matter how many fancy clothes she was given, or how many articles on social etiquette she studied, inside she would still be the same Nicky Bennett. That insecure little girl with holes in her socks.

But she knew how to fake it to make it.

You painted on a smile and acted as if you didn't care.

'Nicola, meet Sebastian and Lydia, my brother and sister,' said Alessio, distracted by a sudden movement which made him glance back towards the house. 'Ah, I see my mother has just arrived and she's on her own. Would you excuse me for a moment?'

'Yes, of course.'

His eyes looked very fierce as he glittered a

warning glance towards his siblings. 'Be nice to her, okay?'

'Alessio!' exclaimed Lydia, in mock horror. 'Would I ever be anything else?'

'Hello,' said Nicola into the silence which followed Alessio's departure, holding out her hand towards Lydia, and producing her best gallery smile. 'How lovely to meet you.'

But Lydia didn't shake it, instead she removed a glass from the tray of a passing waitress and pressed a flute of cold champagne into Nicola's fingers.

'Just to make it clear, we're Alessio's *half* brother and sister,' she elaborated smoothly. 'I don't think we should allow sentiment to get in the way of accuracy, do you? Same mother, different father.' Her eyes darted towards the French windows as if checking Alessio was still out of earshot. 'We were both born securely within wedlock, unlike your wunderkind boyfriend.'

At this point, Sebastian raised his sandy eyebrows. 'You do know he's illegitimate?'

Nicola was so tempted to say *and so am I*, but stopped herself. She wasn't supposed to be trashing her own reputation in order to save Alessio's—who probably didn't need her help anyway. 'Oh, I don't think that kind of thing matters at all any more,' she commented mildly.

'No?'

She saw a disappointed look pass between the pair before Lydia tried a different tack.

'You do realise this is the first time Alessio's ever brought a woman here?' she continued.

'Yes, he told me.'

'I suppose it must be because Papa has relaxed the bedroom rule.'

'I have no idea,' said Nicola, her cheeks flushing in the darkness, and she wished Alessio would come back.

Lydia glanced down at Nicola's left hand. 'Does this mean it's serious? That our famous billionaire sibling has found himself a prospective bride at last? I must say, you weren't a bit what I was expecting, Nicola—given that he usually has a penchant for firecracker brunettes.'

Her critical gaze washed over Nicola, who now was now feeling washed-out and inadequate as she silently compared herself to the vibrant firecrackers.

'I don't usually date men like him either,' she answered evenly.

'So. Tell me a secret.' Lydia took another large mouthful of champagne. 'How on earth do you put up with him?'

'I'm… I'm not sure what you mean.'

'Oh, come on. Isn't he a little *ostentatious* about all his wealth? I keep reading about his plane and his priceless artworks and his high-tech factories. I mean, I'm assuming his PR team make sure they position all that stuff in the press to enhance his reputation, but really…it isn't a terribly *classy* thing to do to keep banging on about how much you own, is it?'

Her verbal demolition was followed by an insincere smile which was making Nicola feel distinctly queasy but suddenly all her own perceived insecurities began to fade in the light of the other woman's words, because they rankled. How dared Lydia be so rude about Alessio in front of someone she'd met for the first time? Yes, her own family might have been dragged up from the gutter, with several members choosing to remain there—but nobody could say they weren't loyal. They all had each other's backs. And suddenly, out of nowhere, came a fierce desire to defend him from his viper-mouthed half-sister. 'I can't imagine for a moment that your brother gets people to plug him or his possessions,' she deflected coolly. 'According to my boss, he's a notoriously private man who likes to keep his life *out* of the papers.'

'Maybe he's got a lot to hide?' suggested Sebastian, with a short laugh.

'Who cares what he wants to keep secret? That's everybody's right, surely? Anyway, maybe it should be the other way round,' Nicola continued doggedly. 'If you turn the question round—how on earth does he put up with *me*? You'll have to ask him. But to spare my blushes, perhaps you'd better not do it within my earshot.'

At that moment Lord Bonner arrived and dinner

was announced, and Nicola was grateful to be led away from the toxic pair towards a table at the far end of the terrace, which was covered in gleaming silverware and sparkling crystal. Tall candles were flickering in the indigo dusk, fireflies were sparking their tiny golden flames and the scent of the starry jasmine flowers was perfuming the air. It looked like a scene from an advert, or a lifestyle magazine—but it was hard to appreciate anything because she could sense a terrible tension bubbling beneath the surface as she took her seat between Alessio and his mother.

And now her inexplicable reaction to his half-sister made Nicola's face grow warm. Had she felt the need to defend him because they'd shared that red-hot moment in the bedroom? Why else would it be? Had their physical closeness helped forge a new kind of bond? But his terse nod of greeting made it clear he didn't share any such feelings and so Nicola sought to lighten the atmosphere around the table which was, after all, what she was being paid to do.

She made small talk. She was good at that. She enthused about the delicious food, which was cooked by the family's resident chef and served by a variety of young women from the nearby village. She sipped a little fine wine—but not too much, knowing she needed all her resolve to line up those cushions later. She needed a similar resolve when first Lydia, and then Lord Bonner attempted to interrogate her about her background. But Nicola was a deft hand at batting away unwanted questions like these and couldn't help notice Alessio's lazy smile as she stonewalled them yet again.

Only once, before *the incident* occurred, which was to derail the whole evening, was she momentarily wrong-footed. A simple dessert of cherries and ice cream was being carried to the table on a silver platter to whoops of childish delight from Lydia and Sebastian, when Alessio's mother suddenly turned to her and asked in a low voice whether her son was happy.

Nicola didn't hesitate. She didn't say she suspected Alessio di Bari was a man fundamentally incapable of happiness, because that was not the answer any mother wanted to hear. There were many different grades of lies, she thought fleetingly—and if there was such a thing, then this was a good one.

'He is,' she said softly, her heart clenching with guilt as the beautiful Italian matriarch gave a trembling smile in response.

'It was worth it, then,' she said.

But Nicola didn't have time to ponder the meaning behind Rosetta's sad words because an unknown guest had suddenly arrived in their midst, followed by a flustered-looking housekeeper. Surrounded by a miasma of cigarette smoke, a statuesque redhead in a tight white dress came to a halt at the far end of the table. She looked at each one of them in turn, leaving Lord Bonner until last. And then she smiled with the look of a starving predator who had just spotted a piece of glistening meat. There was a split second of silence while everyone stared at the glamorous intruder, and then all hell broke loose.

Nicola heard Rosetta gasp and thought Lydia's and Sebastian's eyes were going to pop out of their heads as their father rose to his feet and made his way towards the stunning intruder, like a man who was caught up in the midst of a powerful spell.

'Monica,' he said, but the shock in his aristocratic voice was underpinned with something which sounded remarkably like triumph. 'This is…unexpected.'

'I guess it is.' She lifted one bare, bronzed shoulder and shot him another vermillion smile. 'You always said you wanted to show me your Italian home, so here I am,' she drawled. 'Show me!'

But Alessio was on his feet, too, his face thunderous, his fists white-knuckled and clenched by his sides. He surveyed his stepfather with a mixture of disbelief and contempt as his mother began to quietly cry. 'Get her out of here. *Now*,' he snapped from between gritted teeth and his stepfather nodded, as if unwilling to confront the ire of his furious stepson.

Alessio watched the couple depart before turning to his sister. 'Take Mamma to her room,' he instructed. 'I'll be along to see her in a moment. And, Nicola, go and start packing, will you? We're leaving.'

Nicola gazed at him blankly—but what else could

she do but obey? She waited until Lydia had taken her mother away and only Sebastian was left, having watched the drama unfold, his head turning this way and that, like a spectator at a tennis match.

'Long time coming,' he said, his posh accent unsteady as he picked up his wine glass and drained it in one.

'I wouldn't know,' answered Nicola coldly.

But it seemed surreal to be back upstairs, pulling out all her new and mostly unworn clothes and layering them back into the plush leather suitcase which had also been purchased for this trip. It seemed that her brief tenure as Alessio's paid companion had come to an abrupt end. All that angst about sharing a bed had come to nothing.

Taking off the fairy-tale dress, she pulled on a denim skirt and a shirt and walked over to the window, where the almost full moon had turned the landscape into something magical. But just like magic, none of this was real. The silvery light hid the weeds and snakes which lived in the shadows of the gardens. The seeming perfection was flawed because there was no such thing as perfection. Not in places, nor in people, she reminded herself bitterly. Especially not in people.

She heard the door open and close and when she turned around she saw Alessio standing there, just inside the room, his hard body unmoving. And if she'd thought his expression had been forbidding earlier, that was nothing to the anger which harshened his stony features now. But she wasn't here to analyse or offer an opinion. Matter-of-factness was what he needed, which might remove some of the heat from the situation.

'So, what happens next?' she said calmly.

At the sound of her words, his eyes cleared, as if he had only just remembered he was not alone. 'Just that?' He gave a short laugh. 'No other questions?'

'It's none of my business,' she replied.

'You're not curious about why my stepfather was openly flaunting his mistress in front of his wife?'

She shrugged. 'Even if I was, surely that's irrelevant?'

'*Certo.* Totally irrelevant. But I applaud your attitude, Nicola. Not many women would have resisted the temptation to dig deeper. It's one of the things which made me realise you would be the ideal candidate for what I needed.' His gaze was speculative. 'Your coolness. Your...' He hesitated, as if he could not find the right word in either English or Italian. 'You are an enigma,' he said at last. 'And that's why I felt it safe to employ you.'

Nicola didn't know if she liked the sound of that. He made her sound like a robot, but at least his words reinforced the transactional aspect of their relationship. 'Which brings me back to my original question,' she said crisply. 'What do we do now?'

'We're leaving, of course. I want my mother to come with us, but she is refusing.'

'Can't you…insist?'

'Don't you think I've tried?' he demanded. 'But short of forcibly bundling her in the car, she's going nowhere. She's waiting for my father to "come to his senses".' He gave a bitter laugh. 'And I refuse to hang around to witness any more of her inevitable humiliation. Plus, if the truth were known, I don't trust myself not to hit him, and I am not a violent man.' In the moonlight, his eyes were shards of pure silver. 'Still no questions?' he added roughly.

As his narrowed gaze bored into her, Nicola shook her head. If he thought she was fascinated by his dysfunctional family, he was wrong. Didn't she have one of her own to worry about, which made his look like amateurs? She thought about Callum pacing his prison cell and pregnant Stacey, watching TV in her poky bedsit, and as she realised she had only 'worked' for one afternoon and evening, a wave of anxiety washed over her. Because what if all this had been for nothing?

The words came blurting out in a rush before she could stop them. 'Are you still intending to pay me?'

Did she imagine his look of distaste? No, she was pretty sure she did not—nor the sudden scorn in his voice.

'Oh, yes, Nicola. Have no fear. I will pay you in full.'

'And…we're flying back to England tonight?'

'Unfortunately, no. I've sent the plane back to England and I won't be able to get it back until Monday.'

'Why not?'

'Because I've lent it to my London secretary. Her mother has been sick and they're flying her to France for the weekend.' He shrugged. 'Tomorrow, I can arrange for a commercial airline to take you home—but for tonight, we're going to have to find somewhere to stay.'

Nicola glanced down at her watch, startled to discover it was almost midnight. She swallowed. 'You mean, find a hotel?'

'That would obviously be impossible at this time of year and night,' he returned coolly. 'Fortunately, a friend of mine, Khaled—he's a sheikh actually—has a property up in the hills. It's just over the border, in Tuscany, and it's empty at the moment.' The smile he glittered her was edged with steel. 'We can go there, if you like.'

If she *liked*?

As if she had a choice.

Nicola bit her lip, telling herself this was going to be hell on earth. But no matter how hard she tried, she couldn't deny her sudden flare of excitement as she contemplated spending a night alone with Alessio di Bari.

CHAPTER SEVEN

SECURITY LIGHTS BLOOMED by their feet and sound of barking dogs echoed in the night air as they weaved their way through the cypress-scented grounds, towards a stone cottage. Punching out the code on the keypad, Alessio opened the door and stepped inside.

'What is this place?' Nicola asked as he flicked a switch and light flooded through the room, illuminating the bare walls and deceptively simple furniture.

Alessio's eyes narrowed. 'Not what you imagined?' he suggested sardonically.

Defensively, she shrugged. 'When you said your friend was a sheikh, I naturally assumed—'.

'Something on more palatial lines?'

'Well, yes.'

He put their cases down, assaulted by a sudden stab of recognition as he looked around, for it was a long time since he had stayed somewhere as small as this. Everything was bespoke and high-end, as befitted a property owned by a billionaire sheikh—but there was only so much you could do with dimensions like these and suddenly the fragment of a memory whispered into his mind.

His grandmother's tiny flat above the shop in the village square. The smell of Altamura bread wafting up from the bakery, the steaming pot on the stove and the distant view of the mountains. But his grandmother had left this world all too soon and his heartbreaking farewell to her had made him determined never to let anyone get close to him again. The only woman he had loved and trusted had not been around to enjoy the fruits of his success, cruelly cut down by an illness which had ravaged her. Sorrow mingled with regret and he tensed, because that was the trouble with memory. It dragged you back to places you didn't want to visit.

With an effort he forced his attention back to the matter in hand and met the curious grey eyes of his reluctant companion. 'Khaled offered to have someone open up the main house for us,' he explained. 'But since it's full of priceless artworks and I didn't want security swarming everywhere, I opted for the converted shepherd's hut instead. It's small, but as you see it's supremely comfortable.' He slanted her a look of mocking challenge. 'Any objections?'

'Would there be any point in me objecting?'

'What do you think?'

'I don't imagine you'd like to know what I think.'

A low laugh rumbled from somewhere deep inside him. 'Do you know, I think I prefer you feisty to enigmatic?'

'Which would only be relevant if I were looking for your approval, which I'm not,' she said, glancing around the room like a trapped animal, trying to work out the nearest escape route. 'So why don't I have a look around to see what the rest of the accommodation has to offer?'

'Be my guest.'

Arrested by the peachy curve of her bottom, he watched as she ascended the narrow wooden staircase but returned almost as quickly, not managing to conceal her expression of…

He frowned. He couldn't quite put his finger on it. Was it dread? Maybe. But could dread co-exist with the flash of excitement, or was he simply reading what he wanted to see in her grey eyes?

'What's the matter?'

'Nothing,' she said flatly.

'Bad news on the sleeping front?'

'You could say that. There's…there's only one bedroom and only one bed.'

'Would it reassure you to know that I've spent the majority of my life having to fight women off, not the other way round?' he boasted, before adding softly, 'Control has never been an issue for me.'

He saw her bite her lip before turning her back on him.

'I'm going to investigate the kitchen,' she said. 'See if I can find some tea.'

'Or wine?' he suggested, stretching his arms above his head and stifling a yawn. 'It's been a long day.'

Alessio sank down onto the small but sumptuous sofa before punching out a text to Lydia. He barely heard from his half-sister from one year to the next, and that suited him just fine, but it added to the already bizarre nature of the evening to see her reply come winging straight back.

Mamma's asleep now. Papa and that woman have gone to the gatehouse. You should have stayed, Alessio, you know you should.

Why was that? he wondered cynically. So that she and her brother could abdicate all responsibility while continuing to display their resentment towards him at all times? But a lifetime of deliberately blanking their vitriol made him reply with restraint.

He wrote back.

Whatever you need, let me know. Tell her to speak to my lawyers in the morning.

It was a forlorn hope. But as he slid his phone back into his pocket he found himself thinking about Nicola again, unable to shift the serene image of her face from his memory. Those icy eyes and pale hair and that shuttered way she had of looking at him. Was it her cool attitude which had so captured his imagination, or the erotic flame which had scorched his senses during that single kiss?

The tension between them had been escalating as they had driven through the Tuscan hills, the unmistakable weight of sexual awareness hanging heavy in the air. Surely she must have felt it, too—as tangible as the heat of his blood and fierce beat of his heart. He had waited for some kind of acknowledgement—the subtle brushing of her arm against his perhaps—but she had just stared in silence at the darkened Italian countryside, keeping firmly to her side of the car.

His leant his head back and closed his eyes. He had offered her this job because he'd known she would be perfect for it, but now he recognised there had been more to it than that. She intrigued him. Her aloof manner turned him on—and she had spiked a powerful surge of desire which had lain dormant for so long. But he had meant what he'd said. Control had never been an issue. Just because he wanted to have sex with Nicola Bennett, didn't mean he was going to, for wouldn't that create more trouble than it was worth?

Yet here, in this upmarket cottage with nothing but the velvety darkness outside, he could feel reason being defeated by the irresistible lure of arousal.

He couldn't stop thinking about the way she'd kissed him, or the musky scent of her desire perfuming the air as his fingers had explored her. His throat thickened as he remembered the way she had parted her soft thighs and remembered, too, his idiocy in ignoring that silent invitation. Like some old-fashioned fool he had insisted she open her eyes and look at him. He had wanted her to acknowledge him and say his name—as if that actually *mattered*. And he had broken the enchantment. He had been left hard and full, and frustrated.

Just as he was now.

So deep was he in uncomfortable thought that he didn't hear Nicola return and when he looked up, she was placing a bottle of wine on the streamlined table, along with a single glass and a steaming mug.

'Here,' she said, pushing the bottle and corkscrew towards him.

'You aren't going to join me?'

She shook her head and pointed towards her tea, her voice faintly repressive. 'I'm fine, thanks.'

She sat down beside him, though he noticed that she perched as far away as possible, and he watched as she bent to remove her espadrilles, his gaze inexplicably drawn to her unvarnished toenails.

The wine was good but failed to relax him—and since Nicola's silence provided nothing in the way of diversion, Alessio couldn't stop going back over the evening. The ugliness of his stepfather's triumphant expression and his mother's inevitable tears. Had the festering sore at the centre of their marriage burst open at last, spilling all its poison? he wondered bitterly.

'Why the hell do women put up with toxic relationships?' he demanded suddenly, but naturally Miss Cool didn't react. She just tipped her head to one side and considered his question, as if he'd made a benign enquiry about the weather.

'Usually because they're poor and can't afford to escape.'

Was it her total lack of curiosity which made him pursue the subject further? Or the anger still simmering inside him which needed some kind of outlet? 'My mother isn't poor,' he said flatly. 'If she walked out of that farce of a marriage tomorrow, she'd get a large enough settlement to enable her to live in relative luxury for the rest of her life. Even if she didn't, I'd be happy enough to fund her lifestyle.'

'Maybe she's afraid of being lonely?'

'You think cruelty is preferable to loneliness?' he snapped.

Nicola met the angry blaze of his eyes, taken aback by the brutal candour of his questions, though this wasn't the first time such a thing had happened. Sometimes people came into the gallery and let slip the most extraordinary things and she'd often wondered if it was because powerful billionaires had so few people they could confide in that they turned to

her. Or whether it was a consequence of her ability
to fade into the background—to be quiet and invis-
ible—a convenient sounding board.

Yet this wasn't an anonymous patron, venting his
spleen. She was here because she was being paid.
She and Alessio were trapped together miles from
anywhere and, because she was far from indifferent
to him and all that brooding sexuality, she needed to
put some kind of boundaries in place. She ought to
return to that perfect little kitchen on the pretext of
making more tea—in the hope he might stop asking
these harsh and bitter questions.

But the pain which had hardened his brilliant eyes
was difficult to ignore, and a lifetime of trying to
fix other people made Nicola want to reach out to
him, even though every instinct warned her not to.

'Talking can sometimes be cathartic,' she observed slowly.

Frustratedly, he shook his head. 'I should never
have brought you here and subjected you to such a
damned mess.'

She put her cup down on the table and looked at
him. 'Why *is* it such a mess?'

There was a pause. 'Because my stepfather is a
bully who gets his kicks from humiliating people—
women in particular, though he isn't averse to hurt-
ing children.'

'So why…?' She bit her lip, wondering if he was
talking about himself. 'Why does she stay?'

'Why *do* women stay? I've asked myself the same question all my life—only to come away with the same sense of incomprehension and frustration every time.' His eyes glittered. 'And now the visit for which you have prepared so carefully has been cut short and you find yourself in the unfortunate position of being marooned in the middle of the Italian countryside.'

'That much is true,' Nicola agreed slowly, wishing she could obliterate some of the pain etched upon his beautiful face. She glanced out of the window, where she could see the silvery wash of moonlight glimmering on a distant swimming pool. 'I could think of worse places to get marooned in.'

'What, even with a man you despise?'

Nicola met the taunting question in his eyes, knowing there was plenty about Alessio di Bari *not* to like. He infuriated her with his arrogance and high-handedness, yes, but she remained overwhelmingly attracted to him. She had taken on this bizarre job in order to help her feckless brother and his girlfriend, but something had happened along the way. Something she hadn't planned. With a single kiss the Italian billionaire had changed her, just like that. He had put a match to the bonfire of her senses and set them on fire, branding erotic images on her mind which wouldn't seem to go away.

The slow graze of his fingers creeping up towards her panties.

She swallowed.

More to Love.
More to Explore.

With more to explore, we'd love to send you up to 4 BOOKS, absolutely FREE when you try the Harlequin Reader Service.

They say that "less is more" — but not when it comes to reading your favorite books!

We know that readers like you can't wait to open their newest book and settle down reading.

We feel the same way. That's why today, you can say "YES" to MORE of the great reading you love — absolutely FREE!

Try **Harlequin® Desire** and get 2 books featuring the worlds of the American elite with juicy plot twists, delicious sensuality and intriguing scandal.

Try **Harlequin Presents® Larger-Print** and get 2 books featuring the glamourous lives of royals and billionaires in a world of exotic locations, where passion knows no bounds.

Or **TRY BOTH** and get 2 books from each series!

Your free books are completely free, even the shipping! If you continue with your subscription, you can look forward to curated monthly shipments of brand-new books from your selected series, always at a discount off the cover price! Plus you can cancel any time.

So don't miss out, return your Free Books Claim Card today to get your Free books.

Pam Powers

Free Books Claim Card
Say "Yes" to More Books!

YES! I love reading, please send me more books from the series I'd like to explore and a free gift from each series I select.
Get MORE to read, MORE to love, MORE to explore!

Just write in "**YES**" on the dotted line below then select your series and return this Claim Card today and we'll send your free books & gift asap!

➥ _YES_ ⬅

Which do you prefer?

☐ **Harlequin Desire®**
225/326 HDL GRTM

☐ **Harlequin Presents® Larger-Print**
176/376 HDL GRTM

☐ **BOTH**
225/326 & 176/376
HDL GQ94

FIRST NAME	LAST NAME

ADDRESS

APT.#	CITY

STATE/PROV.	ZIP/POSTAL CODE

EMAIL ☐ Please check this box if you would like to receive newsletters and promotional emails from Harlequin Enterprises ULC and its affiliates. You can unsubscribe anytime.

HD/HP-622-LR_MMM22

HARLEQUIN Reader Service —**Here's how it works:**

▼ If offer card is missing write to: Harlequin Reader Service, P.O. Box 1341, Buffalo, NY 14240-8531 or visit www.ReaderService.com ▼

BUSINESS REPLY MAIL
FIRST-CLASS MAIL   PERMIT NO. 717   BUFFALO, NY

POSTAGE WILL BE PAID BY ADDRESSEE

HARLEQUIN READER SERVICE
PO BOX 1341
BUFFALO NY 14240-8571

NO POSTAGE
NECESSARY
IF MAILED
IN THE
UNITED STATES

The silken throb of her sex as she silently prayed for him to touch her more intimately...

Was it that blissful but ultimately frustrating experience which made her flirt with him, or just a desire to shake off all her responsibilities for once, and see what happened?

'I wouldn't say,' she offered, as lightly as she could, 'that I actually *despised* you.'

At first she thought he hadn't been listening, or had chosen to ignore her words. But when he looked at her... Nicola's heart missed a beat. When he *looked* at her, the pain in his face had become transmuted into something else. Something raw, and sensual and hungry.

'I want to kiss you,' he said, his voice thick. 'That's all I can think about right now. I want to blot out the world and ravish those delicious lips of yours. I want to carry on what we started this afternoon, Nicola—only this time I don't want to stop.'

It was the boldest thing anyone had ever said to her and as the silken heat of sexual awareness whispered over her skin again, Nicola felt dizzy with desire. It was weird. She felt lost and found, all at the same time. But it wasn't just her physical reaction which was so disorientating—it was the accompanying flutter of her thoughts. The absolute certainty that *this* was why she had waited all these years before having sex. Had she known on some subliminal level that Alessio di Bari was going to walk into her life and there was no way she would have wanted anyone but him to be her first lover?

But that was crazy thinking, from a woman who should have known better. If she wanted him, she mustn't frighten him away. She mustn't behave like every other woman in her family by being needy, or desperate. He had said he liked her because she was cool. Wouldn't he be appalled if he knew the real person who existed behind the serene exterior she had so carefully cultivated? The product of one of London's roughest estates, who was still a *virgin*?

She mustn't tell him that either, because she suspected that a man with his degree of experience would be horrified to learn how innocent she was.

But he's going to find out anyway…and then how is he going to react?

She didn't care.

She didn't care about anything right then.

Nicola reached out to touch the hard curve of his jaw, revelling in the rough rasp of new growth which brushed against her palm. Let her—and him—cross that bridge when they came to it. Hadn't she spent her whole life doing things for other people? The only reason she was here was because her brother had got himself into trouble yet again. Why *shouldn't* she have something for herself for once, even if it only lasted one night?

'So go ahead. Kiss me,' she urged, hoping she didn't sound like a faltering novice.

He took the hand which was still resting against his jaw and lifted it to his lips, taking each finger inside his mouth and sucking it. It managed to be innocuous and intensely erotic and Nicola gasped when he drew his mouth away. 'Oh,' she said, and he gave a slow smile as he heard the note of disappointment in her voice.

'I want to undress you. Very, very slowly. But not here. Not on the floor, or on that undersized sofa like a couple of teenagers with no place to go. I want you upstairs, Nicola,' he commanded. 'Now.'

'Okay,' she agreed, as if she regularly received such propositions—trying to blot out her sudden rush of nerves. Her heart was pounding as he led her upstairs and she wondered why he was sounding almost *mechanical*. As if this were more about technique than feelings. As if he took part in this kind of detached seduction all the time.

Did he?

Nicola swallowed. Of course he did—and that was fact, not conjecture on her part. He might try his best to lead a private life but the Internet was full of stories about his conquests—women who were the polar opposite of her. The firecracker brunettes Lydia had spoken about. Women who had everything, while she had nothing.

Shouldn't that be enough to make her have second thoughts?

Probably. Especially as they had now reached the

bedroom and all it symbolised. She stood on the threshold of the room, uncertain what to do, staring across the room at the neatly made bed, covered with exquisite white linen. The sunset was nothing but a memory and bright moonlight was streaming in through the unshuttered windows, coating everything in molten silver. But Alessio's expression was unreadable as he stared down into her face, and Nicola held her breath as she gazed up at him.

Had the journey upstairs been long enough to make him question the wisdom of what they were about to do? Had the billionaire financier suddenly realised he was about to have sex with ordinary Nicky Bennett and she was the last woman he should be holding in his arms?

But then he bent his head to hers and that first touch of his lips was enough to make her senses explode.

Oh, God.

She shivered.

It was like everything she'd read about, only this was for real.

Fire rippled through her veins, warm heat making her dissolve. Her breasts felt as if they were going to burst right out of her shirt and her tummy was tightening. She wanted to touch him. To feel him, and taste him. His arms slid around her waist and as she opened her mouth to him and swayed a little, she thought she felt him smile against her lips.

Should she be more restrained than this? More like the person she was supposed to be? Cool, unflappable Nicola Bennett who never let anything get to her?

But she couldn't.

And neither, it would appear, could he.

Wasn't Alessio di Bari supposed to be the self-professed master of control and wasn't he supposed to be undressing her *very, very slowly*? So why were buttons flying off her shirt so rapidly that she could hear them bouncing their way across the bedroom floor? Her shirt flew open and he slid it from her shoulders, letting it flutter to the ground in a silken whisper. He stared down at her, his eyes narrowed and smoky as her breasts strained towards him, pushing furiously against the black lace.

'Now that,' he murmured, 'is an invitation I can't refuse.'

He bent his head to trail his lips over her breasts and she tipped her head back.

'Ohh...' Nicola moaned as his teeth expertly grazed over the lace-covered nipples. Was that really her voice she could hear? She was being so uncharacteristically loud. So *vocal* and *uninhibited*. But that was her last rational thought, because Alessio was undoing the buttons of her denim skirt and it was concertinaing to the ground, so that she was left wearing nothing but her bra and knickers.

'You are even more beautiful than I imagined,' he

husked, his gaze raking over her silky black panties, slung low on her hips.

'I'm not.'

'Yes, you are,' he contradicted, tilting his chin so that their gazes were locked on a collision course. 'I'm not going to tell you any lies tonight, Nicola Bennett.' His lips hardened, his eyes gleaming cold in the moonlight—as steely as the sudden edge to his next words. 'Even if at times you might wish that I did.'

CHAPTER EIGHT

'I'M NOT GOING to tell you any lies tonight.'

Alessio's words echoed round the bedroom and set faint alarm bells ringing but Nicola ignored them. All she could think about was this. *This.* She was going to have sex for the first time, after a lifetime of never having been interested before. She'd never even been alone in a bedroom with a man before yet she didn't feel in the least bit shy, despite being almost naked. How could she feel shy, when Alessio was gazing at her like that—the way she'd seen him look at pictures in her boss's gallery, his brilliant eyes smoky with appreciation?

Yet he still had his clothes on and she wasn't sure what to do next. What was the dress code—or rather, the *undress* code? Should she be touching *him*? She was terrified of messing up, of betraying her woeful inexperience—of disappointing, not just him, but herself. Because she'd waited too long to want to screw this up.

But surely she was capable of removing his shirt with some degree of skill. Sliding her fingers over his silk-covered chest, she started popping tiny buttons open. His torso tensed and she could hear his ragged breathing as she undid the shirt in silence, to reveal all the hard, silken flesh beneath. The garment whispered from his shoulders, joining her own on the floor before she bent her lips to his nipple, just as he had done to her.

'Nicola,' he said unsteadily as she circled the nub of puckered flesh with the flick of her tongue.

That sounded like approval, she thought, and was just about to turn her attention to the other one when he tangled his fingers in her hair and tipped her head back so that their eyes were locked on a collision course.

'No. Not like this,' he grated, his breathing still heavy.

Her heart beat with anxiety. 'Is something wrong?'

'Don't ask disingenuous questions,' he reprimanded sternly. 'I want you horizontal. I want to see all that golden hair spread over my pillow.'

He picked her up—he actually *picked her up*—and carried her over to the bed, laying her down on top of it so that she could watch as he undressed. His hand was moving to his zip and Nicola felt a sudden lump in her throat at the thought of seeing an aroused man for the first time in her life. But she wasn't going to waste a second with nerves or shyness, because sex was a natural part of life. She remembered the woman in the painting at the gallery—the way her face had been flushed with sensuality and satisfaction, and she wanted that, too.

She watched Alessio remove his trousers to reveal the silky boxer shorts but couldn't hold back her faint exclamation when she saw the formidable length of his erection—so pale and proud against his dark olive skin. It ran the risk of betraying her inexperience, but the strangled sound seemed to give him immense satisfaction, because he smiled as he came over to the bed and pulled her against his warm flesh.

'Yes, I am big,' he said, quite seriously, as his hardness pressed against her stomach. Reaching inside her panties, he brushed a featherlight fingertip over her quivering flesh. 'But you are so wet. So ready for me. I will not hurt you, Nicola.'

Nicola responded by covering his mouth with kisses and his laugh was low as he unclipped her bra, her breasts tumbling out into his waiting hands. And now he was sliding off her panties and she didn't know how much she could take as he continued to stroke her, with that barely-there touch of his finger.

'Please,' she whimpered as he increased the speed of his movements, making her soar towards something nebulous and sweet. 'Please…'

A spiral of intense pleasure was twisting inside her, like a wire being tightened and tightened and yet still it wasn't enough. When she writhed impatiently, he increased the pressure—fingering the slick flesh until she didn't think she could bear any more. And then suddenly she broke free, crying out her disbelief as she clung to him. As her body began to clench, her last rational thought right then was that he held her completely in his power and that, worryingly, she *liked* it. It didn't make her feel weak—it made her feel strong. Stronger than she'd ever felt before.

'Wow,' he murmured, after a moment, his lips drifting across her head to bury themselves in her hair. 'Who knew that the cool Miss Bennett could be so responsive?'

Through her blissful haze, Nicola felt him pull away from her. 'Oh,' she objected, in a heavy, slurred voice.

'This part is vital, *cara*. But don't worry. I won't be long.'

Nicola watched as he removed a condom from his discarded jeans and a feeling of horror swept over her as she realised she hadn't even checked whether he'd been carrying protection. What if he hadn't? Would she still have let him go ahead? The terrible thought swam into her mind that, yes, she *actually thought she might*—and the irony of that didn't escape her. Was she, who had always been so critical of other people's failings when it came to unprotected sex, not quite as strong-minded as she'd always considered herself to be?

But now all she could think about was the naked

man who was getting back into bed, his powerful limbs gleaming in the moonlight. Restlessly, she writhed as he stroked on the protection, his mercurial eyes glinting with provocation.

'Impatience isn't a trait I would have associated with you,' he murmured.

It wasn't a trait she would have associated with herself, but all Nicola's usual certainties seemed to have vanished. He moved over her, his warm weight pinning her against the mattress, and as she tilted her hips in silent invitation it became important that she acknowledge him. To do something she had consciously refused to do before, for reasons which now seemed insane. As the blunt tip of his erection brushed against her molten heat, she gazed up into the charcoaled silver of his features and her heart pounded.

'Alessio,' she said unsteadily.

His eyes narrowed as if he had recognised the significance of the word.

'That's the first time you've ever said my name,' he observed.

As she nodded, his palm curved around her hip, anchoring it with careless possession. 'Had you been waiting for such a moment as this, Nicola?' he murmured. 'Is this all it would have taken? If I'd done this to you sooner, would you have whispered it? If I'd locked the gallery door and pulled you into the back room and taken you up against the wall behind that bronze statue, with your panties around your ankles, would you have said my name then?'

If she'd been hoping for romance it seemed she was to be disappointed, but somehow the Italian's gritted words were turning her on even more. So that what was intended to be a protest at his audaciousness came out as a shuddered repetition of his name and his own moan sounded almost helpless as he entered her.

And Nicola realised that he *had* lied to her, because it *did* hurt. He was so big and she was so tight that she couldn't hold back her startled gasp of pain. She saw Alessio's smile disappear, his look of disbelief turning into one of grim recognition, and for one awful moment she wondered if he was going to stop and she would never know what it was like. The fleeting thought occurred to her that she might die without ever making love properly.

But he didn't stop.

He just carried on, but now his movements seemed governed by deliberation, rather than the mindless passion of before. Little by little, he eased himself further into her body and little by little her muscles stretched to accommodate him, until he had buried himself so deeply it felt as if he were touching her heart.

His thrusts were slow and careful and despite it being the most amazing thing which had ever happened to her, she was aware of him watching her.

As if he were an observer rather than a participant. Did that matter? Even if it did, Nicola was powerless to fight what was happening as sensation began to bombard her. Did he realise she was close to that mindless release all over again? Was that why he increased his rhythm, so that she was caught up in a frenzy of excitement?

'Alessio,' she whimpered, as wave after wave of bliss swamped her.

Only this time he wasn't listening—he was too intent on his own pleasure. His eyes were closed and his hard features shuttered as his body shuddered out its own release. She lay beneath him, trying to recover her breath along with her composure—but that wasn't easy when Alessio was still pulsing inside her. But this was exactly where she wanted him. She wanted him to stay inside her for ever.

Yet something was urging her to reclaim some of the power she had acceded to him and she sucked in a deep breath of resolve. Everything Nicola had learned in life had been by observing other people's reactions, because she didn't trust her own not to let her down. But if this silence continued much longer, she would start to fill it with her own worst imaginings. Or his. She didn't want him worrying that she was going to regard this as a big deal and reminded herself that she wasn't some hapless little victim. She had come into this with her eyes wide open—well, not all the time, obviously—and Alessio needed to know that.

'Are you disappointed?' she questioned slowly.

'Am I *disappointed*?' He pulled away and frowned. 'Wow. I've been asked a lot of questions after sex, Nicola—but that one is definitely a first.'

'How reassuring to discover that I can be original, even if I am just one of a crowd!'

Her cool words washed over him and Alessio felt a mixture of amusement and curiosity. Usually, he couldn't wait to roll off a woman's body and distance himself, yet for once he wanted to stay buried in her silken sweetness. But since avoiding pregnancy was the most important consideration of all, he carefully withdrew before turning back, his body tightening as he surveyed the wildness of her blonde hair spreading over the pillow, just like every fantasy he'd ever had about her. He tried—and failed—to reconcile the unflappable Nicola Bennett with the sweet virgin who had given him her innocence. He wondered why she had chosen to frame her question so negatively, instead of gushing out the breathless praise which always fell on his ears at such a moment.

Because the sex had been exceptional. Even for him. No, especially for him, he conceded reluctantly. Her swift transformation from ice to fire had first surprised him, then blown his mind. He had been entranced by her. He could never remember feeling so exquisitely aroused as when he had pushed into her molten heat. But there had been another surprise waiting…and Alessio was a man who was rarely surprised—especially in the bedroom. 'Why on earth would I be disappointed?' he drawled.

'Isn't it obvious?' There was a pause, which he had no intention of filling, before she gave an awkward shrug. 'Because I didn't tell you—'

'That you were a virgin?'

She nodded.

Alessio nodded. This kind of analysis was abhorrent to him, but she *was* inexperienced and maybe he needed to take that into account. It was better to ensure she wasn't harbouring any hopes which could never be realised—at least, not by him. He had been accused of many things by women—but falsely dangling the prospect of happily-ever-after had never been among them. But then, he'd never had sex with a virgin before. His heart missed a heavy beat. Nor expected to enjoy it quite so much.

'That would only be a problem if it were significant,' he drawled. 'If, for example, you thought I was so blown away by your innocence—which, incidentally, I was—that I would immediately demand you marry me. Well, then, *sì*, I would be disappointed. And so would you, for that matter, *cara*, because that's not going to happen. Not now, not ever.'

'Let me guess…because every woman you go to bed with is desperate to get your ring on her finger?'

Unapologetically, he shrugged. 'This I cannot deny.'

'Which I suppose implies that having a colossal ego must top the list of most women's marital requirements?'

He gave a slow smile. 'I don't think it's the size of my ego which accounts for my popularity with the opposite sex, *cara*.'

'Oh!'

He could feel waves of indignation radiating towards him, meshing with the far more tangible ripples of desire which were making him want to kiss her again. Tangling his fingers in the silky ropes of her hair, he pulled her towards him and her lips trembled as he grazed his own against them. 'Stop focussing on the unimportant,' he instructed huskily.

'I suppose you're going to tell me what *is* important?'

'You know damned well what's important.'

'How can I, when this is the first time I've ever done this?'

'Then why don't I tell you? Hmm? I want to be inside you again. I want to fill you completely until you can feel nothing else but me. I want to hear you cry my name when you come, like you did just now. That breathless little moan which seemed to go on for ever.' His voice dipped. 'Don't you want that, too, Nicola?'

She blinked at him—as if she couldn't believe quite how explicit he was being, but her eyes were wide and dark, the words rushing from her lips, as if she couldn't hold them back any longer. 'Yes. Yes, I do,' she whispered. 'I want that very much.'

This time he touched her with a deliberate lack of speed, though never had his control been quite so tested. Not a single inch of her flesh did he leave unexplored—first by his fingers and then his lips. Her body was so streamlined, he thought hungrily. So...*perfect*. He watched as her nipples hardened into silver bullets in the moonlight. He stroked his fingertips over soft, slender thighs which parted for him, and when he placed his mouth against her silken core, he could taste her honeyed musk.

As she whimpered beneath the flicker of his tongue, he could feel something unfamiliar—an alien sensation which rolled over him like a heavy wave and threatened to pull him under. Dampening down his own needs, he concentrated solely on hers, but by the time she pulsed helplessly beneath his tongue Alessio could deny himself no longer. His hands were unsteady as he eased on a condom and thrust into her waiting heat. Had he ever been this hard before? he wondered dazedly. Had he ever buried himself so deeply in a woman that it was difficult to know where he ended and she started? Pleasure caught him in a ruthless vice and his cry was wild as the seed pumped from his body.

He must have fallen asleep—unheard of—because when he opened his eyes, the milky wash of a golden dawn was lighting the horizon. Her skin and hair gilded by the rising sun, Nicola was lying on the far edge of the bed with her back to him, but her posture told him she was awake. And even though he had convinced himself he didn't care enough to pursue this particular topic, he broke the rule of a lifetime by doing exactly that.

'So why?' he questioned, stretching his arms above his head and giving a lazy yawn.

Nicola had been lying there wide-eyed while Alessio slept, preparing her answers for questions like these, like an ambitious pupil swotting for an exam. She turned to face him, unable to prevent the instant clutch of desire on seeing him naked against the snowy bedding.

The most important thing she needed to remember was that this fling was going nowhere—and not just because he lived in Manhattan and she in London. Or because he was an eligible billionaire and she nothing but a glorified shopgirl. There wasn't going to be any kind of future for a couple like them, so why spoil what they had now with harsh reality? He wasn't really interested in her sexual history, or, indeed, any kind of history. He was probably only asking to be polite, or to pass the time. After all, they had to talk about *something* in between orgasms.

So she pushed away the kittenish mood which seemed to have crept up on her, the one which wanted to purr that she'd been waiting all her life for a man like him. Imagine how that would go down!

'You mean, why was I a virgin?' she verified slowly. 'Or why did I choose you?'

'Both.'

She didn't miss the brief nod of his head—as if her measured response was reassuring, making her think she'd pitched it just right. All she needed to do was to convince him that she wasn't going to read too much into this. 'I guess I was too busy with my career to have any time for men,' she answered truthfully, but didn't elaborate. She didn't tell him she'd been determined to avoid the social norms of the run-down estate where she'd been brought up, where relationships meant bust-ups and money problems. Bruised eyes and unplanned pregnancies. Or to tell him that her independence was vital to her and she was determined to never rely on men as her mother had done.

Because none of those things were relevant.

'You haven't answered the second part,' he observed.

Nicola hesitated. Neither was she going to tell him he was the most gorgeous man she'd ever met and it would have been easier to have stopped breathing than to have resisted his kiss. Would he be appalled to learn that she had melted a little to discover he'd lent his plane to his secretary for her sick mother? Probably. He might even accuse her of sentimentality, because lending a plane would mean nothing to a man like him. She could also confess that her heart had gone out to him after witnessing those awful scenes at his mother's house, but he might interpret that as pity. And Nicola despised pity—a smug emotion she'd been subjected to often enough in the past.

So she swept her fingers back through her tousled hair and told him a different type of truth—a statement she wouldn't have dreamed of sharing twenty-four hours ago. But what was the point of being naked in bed with someone if you couldn't say some of the things which were on your mind?

'Obviously, as time went on and everyone was—'

'Falling by the wayside?' he mocked.

'I wasn't making any moral judgements!' she answered quietly. 'But as I saw more and more of my friends having sex, I started wondering if I was missing out. I suppose I decided I needed a bit of an... an education.'

He still wasn't reacting.

'I w-wanted to find out if it lived up to all the hype,' she concluded, her stumbled words filling the awkward silence. 'That's all.'

'That's all,' he echoed, fixing her with a curious gaze.

She saw the cold calculation which entered his eyes and wondered if she'd imagined his fleeting look of disappointment.

'And was it as good as you thought it was going to be?'

'Even better!' she said, with a rare fervour, and he laughed.

'You know, you really are turning out to be something of a surprise, Nicola Bennett,' he murmured. 'You make me want to do it to you all over again.'

'And what's…what's stopping you?' she questioned, with shy bravado.

'Nothing. In fact, I intend making love to you for as long as possible.' Pushing a handful of hair away from her face, he guided her hand towards one hair-roughened thigh. 'Though if you're still intending to catch that commercial flight in the morning, it's going to eat into the time we have together.' Curling her fingers around his growing erection, he pressed his lips to her ear. 'So why don't you stay on a little longer?'

CHAPTER NINE

OF *COURSE* NICOLA didn't catch the commercial flight the next morning. Instead she eked out every last moment with the Italian billionaire. For two days and three nights, Alessio gave her a taste of paradise—there was no other way to describe it—and she wasn't someone with an overactive imagination. Yet even in her wildest dreams she had never imagined sex could be like this, or that she was capable of experiencing such pleasure, over and over again.

'You know—you are very, very good,' Alessio growled at one point, when she was straddling him on the very sofa they had rejected as too small the previous evening.

'You almost make that sound like a complaint,' she murmured, the experimental thrust of her hips making him groan helplessly.

'*Dio*. Are you out of your mind?' His smoky sapphire gaze burned into her. 'You are an exceptionally fast learner, Nicola.'

Yes. She always had been. It had been one of the things which had helped her leave her humble beginnings behind. And one of the first things she'd learnt was always keep your expectations realistic. So that when Alessio captured her lips and she shattered into pieces yet again, she didn't start imagining what this would be like on a permanent basis. Because that was never going to happen. None of this was real. She didn't really know him and he didn't know her. She didn't want him to. She was having fun in this delicious vacuum. She had pushed her worries about Stacey and the baby and her brother's release from her mind. She had left her cares back in England. Why shouldn't she enjoy this sense of freedom and this brand-new version of herself?

Which was why she kept her face impassive as their plane began its descent towards London and Alessio told her of his plans.

'As soon as we land, I'm afraid I'm going to have to leave you. I have a business meeting in the city.' There was a pause. 'And tomorrow I must fly back to the States.'

'That's okay.' Nicola smiled reassuringly. 'No worries.'

His sapphire eyes had narrowed. 'You're sure?'

What did he imagine she was going to do? she wondered caustically. Cling to his ankles and refuse to let go, just because they'd spent the last forty-eight hours having non-stop sex in the beautiful Italian countryside?

And isn't that what you'd secretly like to do—hold onto him and never let him go? Aren't you going to miss those long days and nights, with Alessio feeding you scraps of delicious food which had been delivered every morning by some unseen servant of his rich sheikh mate?

'I think I'll just about be able to cope,' she offered wryly.

His answering look conveyed both surprise and approval and Nicola realised that her refusal to try to pin him down was one of the things which made her attractive to him. He was a man who liked the chase, she recognised. An alpha male. A hunter. Maybe it was that which prompted his next drawled statement.

'But I'm going to be in London next week,' he said.

She wondered if he could hear the fierce beating of her heart as she attempted not to sound too delighted. Or too eager. 'Oh, yeah?'

Reluctantly, Alessio removed his hand from where it had been resting deliciously on her knee. There it was again—that familiar indifference. But whereas before her attitude had irritated him, now he was finding it beguiling. It added to her considerable allure and it was turning him on. In fact, *she* was turning him on, just by sitting there. He sucked in an unsteady breath. *Especially* by sitting there, with the sunlight streaming in through the aircraft window and transforming her hair into a shimmering cascade of gold.

He had planned to bid her a civilised farewell once they landed. Maybe give the Mayfair gallery a swerve for a while—at least until things had calmed down, which would obviously be the most sensible outcome. He'd even contemplated sending her something as a memento, because what woman didn't appreciate a new piece of jewellery? Grey diamonds, perhaps—to match her remarkable eyes. But now that the moment of parting had arrived, he was curiously reluctant to end things. At least, just yet.

As she gazed back at him with that unruffled expression, he found himself wanting to shatter her composure. To see her come apart in his arms. He hadn't yet had enough of her, he realised hungrily. Not nearly enough.

'Why don't I take you out for dinner some time?' he said.

The pause which followed would surely have insulted any man—but especially a man who was unused to being kept waiting. But eventually, she inclined her head in a manner which was almost regal. 'Okay. Call me.'

Call me? Alessio could feel the urgent beat of his pulse and wondered if she was playing games with him. Didn't she realise he was aching so much right now that he wanted to dismiss the crew and tiptoe his fingers up her leg and push her panties aside, and…

'Alessio?' She was looking at him, mild concern in her eyes. 'Is something wrong? You almost look as if you're in pain.'

'Nothing's wrong,' he growled. 'I'll get my driver to drop you off at home.'

'No, honestly, I'll get the Tube.'

'I *said*, my driver will drop you off,' he repeated, with an impatient frown. 'There's a chauffeur-driven car at your disposal. Why do you have a problem accepting a simple favour, Nicola?'

Nicola wondered what he would say if she told him. If she explained she was frightened of getting used to this way of living. To his fancy cars and private jets. To *him*. Because wouldn't that make it harder to deal with when it ended—as end it must? She touched the sleeve of her silk dress, her fingertips whispering over the delicate fabric. So many beautiful garments which had gone unworn because they'd spent almost every moment naked. And he had paid for them, she remembered guiltily. He had clothed her from head to foot. Did that make her beholden to him in some way? 'What shall I do with the clothes?' she said.

He frowned. 'You keep them, of course. What else would you do with them?' His phone began to ring and, although he didn't pick up, he gestured towards the cabin door—clearly eager to get away. 'Come on. Let's go.'

At the foot of the aircraft, he deposited a brief, hard kiss on her lips, before opening the door of one of the waiting cars for her. She turned to see him slide into a second vehicle and lift his hand in a gesture of farewell as it pulled away. But he didn't look back, she noticed. His dark head was bent. He was already busy with something. A powerful man with more on his mind than a casual, sexual fling.

Despite his insistence, Nicola had the car drop her off at the nearest Tube station, and despite the driver's protestations that his boss had ordered him to deliver her directly to her front door. But that was the last thing she wanted. Alessio didn't have her address and that was how she wanted to keep it.

'I won't tell if you don't tell,' she said with a conspiratorial smile before ducking into the entrance of the London underground. Once home, she changed into jeans and a T-shirt and went round to see Stacey—panicking slightly when her brother's girlfriend regarded her with dull eyes. Weren't pregnant women supposed to be all glowing with health, with bouncing hair and bright eyes? The tiny bedsit felt stuffy in the oppressive summer heat and Nicola opened up all the windows before making a pot of ginger tea.

'I've got the money,' she announced, emerging from the poky bathroom, which she had briefly spritzed.

Stacey's face was sullen. 'Can't I have it now?'

'The thing is that it's supposed to be for you *and* the baby.' Nicola smiled encouragingly. 'So why don't we go looking for a new place together and you can plan your new home for when Callum is released?'

Stacey shrugged. 'S'pose.'

In a way, it was a relief for Nicola to get back to work and a routine which didn't give her a lot of time to think. By day she worked at the gallery and in the evenings she and Stacey checked out accommodation. Some options were way better than others, but by the following week they had found a clean, modern flat close to a nursery and park. With the proceeds of her Tuscan weekend, they bought a crib, bedding and a stack of tiny baby clothes, which were stored in the brand-new chest of drawers which Nicola managed to put together herself, even though the instructions were pretty incomprehensible. She visited her brother in prison and showed him pictures of the new place, and for the first time in a long time she saw him smile. He gave her a beautiful little wooden teddy bear he had carved in one of his rehabilitation classes, and asked her to give it to Stacey.

The relentless activity kept her days filled and she was often so tired when she went to bed at night that she fell asleep as soon as her head hit the pillow. But there was only so much displacement therapy she could do before the questions she'd buried in the recesses of her mind started to nag away at her.

Alessio had said he would see her this week and she hadn't heard from him.

Of course she hadn't. Was she a complete idiot? The sex had been convenient because they'd been trapped in a remote Italian cottage, but now he was back in his Manhattan playground and able to date his preferred movie star, or model—why *would* he bother contacting her? It had just been a polite way of saying goodbye.

On the plus side, she sold four paintings in quick succession and Sergio told her she was a genius.

'Hiring you was the smartest move I ever made,' he said thoughtfully. 'And the most incredible thing is that you're entirely self-taught.'

'Thanks,' she answered serenely.

But then, Alessio rang. A number she didn't recognise flashed onto her screen and every instinct she possessed urged her to let it go to voicemail.

She picked it up. 'Hello.'

'Nicola.'

She closed her eyes, an unsteady sigh escaping her lungs. How could that single word—that velvety version of her name—make heat instantly rush to her breasts like this? 'Alessio,' she said huskily.

'Ah! For a moment there I thought you were going to pretend you didn't recognise my voice.'

'And why would I do that?'

'Isn't feigned disinterest supposed to keep a man *on his toes*?' he mocked.

'Since we've already established that the sum of my experience with men could be written on the back of a postage stamp—how do you honestly expect me to answer that question?'

He laughed. 'I'll be in London on Friday.' He paused. 'Are you going to have dinner with me?'

Oh, God. Just the thought of it was making her pulse skyrocket. She caught a glimpse of her reflection and saw the huge, almost wild darkening of her eyes. Did he have this power over *all* women? she wondered helplessly. Could he make their bodies melt with desire, just by exchanging a few careless words on the telephone?

Tell him you're busy. Tell him there's no point. Remind him that you live on opposite sides of a huge ocean.

'Sure,' she said casually. 'I'll have dinner with you. Text me a time and a place and I'll meet you there, same as last time.'

He gave a sigh. 'Must we really go through this cat-and-mouse routine again, Nicola?'

She heard the faint impatience in his voice but had no intention of budging, because she needed to keep fantasy and real life separate. She *had* to. Because what if he wanted to come back to her place after dinner, to stay the night? Could she really imagine the powerful billionaire grappling with her plastic shower curtain? 'That's what I want, Alessio,' she said calmly.

But on Friday, a customer spent so long deliberating over a painting, that it was almost seven by the time Nicola closed up the gallery and she was running late. Casting a frantic look at her watch, she went to find her handbag. It was going to be a rush to get back to Peckham in time to change, but she should just about make it in time. Though, come to think of it…she picked up her phone and stared at the blank screen with a stab of disappointment. Alessio still hadn't texted her to tell her where to meet him.

And then, in that uncanny way which sometimes happened—of technology echoing your thoughts—a text came pinging through.

I've booked the Starlight Room at the Granchester for eight p.m.

Gosh. Nicola blinked. That was a bit *public*, wasn't it? She'd heard that the famous indigo ceilings studded with twinkling constellations made the lighting subdued, but there were always paparazzi lurking around the entrance, eager to snap the privileged clientele enjoying the hotel restaurant's exemplary food and wine list. Did he really want to take her *there*?

The gallery bell sounded and Nicola paused, rather irritated at someone ringing on the door, when it was obvious they were closed. But she couldn't just ignore it. The building was secure, but with so many valuable pieces on the premises you could never be too sure. Her finger hovering over the alarm button, she peered out into the golden summer evening, her heart missing a beat when she saw the distinctive figure silhouetted against the plate-glass window.

She darted back out of view, her heart now pounding. What the hell was *he* doing here?

Her text pinged again and she knew who it was from even before she'd looked at the message.

Open the door, cara. I know you're in there.

This was unacceptable. Completely and utterly unacceptable. Marching across the gallery, Nicola unlocked the door and stood glaring at him, trying not to be affected by his powerful presence. But the evening sunlight was making the dark gold of his skin seem even more luminescent than usual, contrasting vividly with the coal-dark hair and sapphire gleam of his eyes.

'What are you doing here?' she demanded.

'Isn't it obvious? I wanted to see you.'

'But you were going to see me anyway. We have a dinner date in exactly…' She glanced down at her watch before lifting her gaze again. 'One hour's time.'

'I couldn't wait that long.'

'Alessio—'

'Let me in, Nicola. Please.'

That final sexy plea was her undoing, and even though she despised herself for her acquiescence, Nicola did just that—though her fingers were trembling as she locked the door behind him before studying the arresting beauty of his face. 'You can't just… turn up like this, without warning.'

'I just did.'

'Why?'

'Because I want to kiss you.'

'Well, you can't.'

'You don't want me to?'

'There's CCTV.'

'Everywhere?'

'Not in the back, no. Alessio…'

'Shh. Just show me, *cara. Show* me.' He linked her fingers with his and she was leading him—she was actually *leading him*—towards the darkened recess at the rear of the gallery. As her footsteps faltered beside the bronze sculpture—which still hadn't sold—he pulled her into his arms and looked down at her, his bright blue gaze piercing through her rapidly crumbling defences. Could he detect her hunger for him? Was that why his lips grazed hers so lightly that a helpless shudder erupted from her lips, before he covered them with the kind of hard and possessive kiss she'd spent the last week dreaming about?

'Alessio,' she gasped, when at last she came up for air.

'Mmm…?' His lips were against her neck, his

breath warm against her skin as he levered her up against the wall.

'We—' she whispered as he began to ruck up her skirt, but already her thighs were parting for him '—mustn't.'

'Do you want me?'

'Yes,' she gasped breathlessly as she skated her fingertips hungrily over his chest.

Alessio greeted her remark with a low laugh of triumph, but he realised that his hands were unsteady as he undid her black skirt and let it pool to the floor. His fingertips brushed against her moist panties and she moaned as he slid them over her hips. As they floated down to join her skirt, he unzipped himself and never had he felt so big, or so hard. 'Do you want me?' he questioned again, but her urgent kiss was answer enough.

'Yes,' she crooned against the thrust of his tongue.

He dealt with the condom—bitterly resenting the time-wasting element of having to protect himself and that realisation provoked a flicker of incomprehension. But then he was lifting up her legs and wrapping them around his hips and all his reservations were forgotten as he pushed inside her. Deep inside her. He swallowed. *Madre di Dio.* It was *incredible. Incredible.* Had any woman ever felt as tight as this?

Somehow he slowed the pace down—even though the primitive need to spill his seed was threatening to overwhelm him. Every sinew in his body was taut as he thrust into her body, until she began to come— making a series of small cries as she spasmed around him. And then he surged inside her, with soft words torn from his lips in a voice which didn't sound like his own.

It took a long time for him to move. He wanted to remain exactly where he was, lost in the slowly receding waves of satisfaction, but they couldn't stay like this all evening…because this was very definitely not his style.

'So. Now what?' he questioned throatily.

Nicola didn't answer—the intense pleasure still washing over her literally making her unable to speak. She couldn't believe she had responded to him like that—so rapidly and so…

She swallowed.

So shamelessly.

Had she really just had sex *at her place of work*? What if Sergio had returned unexpectedly, or if the *unusual* activity in the rear of the gallery had alerted the central security system to the possibility of a trespasser on the premises? She could hardly protest that Alessio di Bari was a bona fide gallery customer, when his clothing was in such telltale disarray and there was the small matter of the empty condom wrapper lying on the floor.

Her heart was pounding as she let her legs slide to the ground, relieved to feel the earth beneath her feet again. As the potent aftermath began to recede she wondered how she could have been so stupid. All her life—*all her life*—she had worked hard to find a job like this—yet she had been prepared to risk it all for a quick thrill with a man who regarded her as nothing but a temporary diversion.

But any anger she felt she would direct at herself, not him. She had wanted that urgent coupling just as much as he had, and she didn't have a clue what to do next. What on earth was she supposed to *say*? Recognising the need to maintain her dignity, she began scooping up her crumpled clothes. 'I need to freshen up,' she said.

Alone in the lavish bathroom which her boss had installed during the gallery's recent refurbishment, she did the best she could with the limited resources available, thankful for the luxurious toiletries which were always kept there. Removing the clips from her updo, she gave it a brisk brush—because at least the thick curtain of hair gave her something to hide behind.

Afterwards, when Alessio wordlessly took her place, she went to the office and busied herself with emails which could have easily waited until Monday, but at least they kept her teeming thoughts occupied, so that when a shadow fell over the desk it took her almost by surprise. And so did the way Alessio levered her to her feet and lifted her fingers to his mouth, grazing his lips over them in a way which made her shiver with desire. But if that curiously old-fashioned gesture disarmed her, his next words put her instantly on her guard.

'My car is outside.'

'And?'

'I'll give you a lift home.' His gaze roved over her white blouse—now a little creased—and her black pencil skirt, and his slow smile was speculative. 'I assume you'll want to get changed before dinner? I'll get them to put the table back.'

A disturbing thought flew into Nicola's mind. Had he deliberately come here to seduce her so that afterwards he could snoop around to see where she lived? This was followed by an impatient sigh, because that really *was* being paranoid. As if he cared! As if he'd even given her that much thought. So take back control. Tell him what *you* want, rather than obediently doing what he says all the time. 'To be honest, I don't want that at all. Too much of a rush,' she explained, with a quick glance at her watch. 'Can't you cancel the booking?'

'Of course I can. Though most people wouldn't pass up on a table at the Starlight.' His blue eyes glinted from between shuttered ebony lashes. 'Unless you have something better in mind?'

'Obviously nothing's going to top one of London's most famous restaurants,' she said. 'But we could always go and...' Nicola shrugged, momentarily distracted by his bright gaze and trying not to read too much into what had just happened. But he had come to find her, hadn't he? He had even said that he couldn't wait until eight o'clock, which was a pretty big admission from a man like him.

So didn't that alter things, if only a bit? She had tasted his luxurious billionaire lifestyle—maybe it was time he sampled hers. And yes, it might emphasise the huge material differences between them, but surely it would also put them on a more equal footing. 'We could always...' She hesitated. 'Eat a sandwich in the park?'

'Eat a sandwich in the park,' he repeated, as if she had just suggested a solo mission to the moon.

'Why not? It's a lovely sunny evening and...well, autumn will be upon us before you know it.' Her confidence growing, she picked up her handbag, unable to deny her pleasure at seeing that look of bemusement crossing over his face. 'There's a great deli on the corner of Maddox Street. Come on, Alessio. Play your cards right and I'll treat you.'

CHAPTER TEN

THE FAINT HUM of traffic was louder than the bird-
song, but the air was warm, the evening was golden
and for the first time in a long time, Alessio felt completely relaxed. Sated by sex and food, he stretched
his arms above his head, his attention caught by the
sight of Buckingham Palace, which stood at the far
end of the park. But the gilded gates and imposing
structure of the majestic building were far less arresting than the sight of the woman perched on the
ground opposite him, her bottom nestling snugly on
his suit jacket.

He narrowed his eyes, still faintly disconcerted
by the position in which he now found himself. Had
he really removed that expensive piece of clothing
and thrown it carelessly onto the dusty ground for
her to sit on? Indeed, he had. His throat dried as his
gaze moved over her. She had kicked off her sensible
work shoes and suddenly he found himself fixated
by the sight of her bare calves. It was crazy. Just a

short while ago his fingers had been inching up her legs towards her panties, yet now those slender ankles seemed to exemplify a very different but equally potent kind of eroticism.

The evening was, he acknowledged wryly, turning out like no other. Instead of enjoying the splendour of the Granchester Hotel's world-famous restaurant, he had eaten a crab sandwich on rye, followed by a punnet of strawberries, while sitting beneath the dappled shade of a London plane tree. And for once, Nicola Bennett didn't appear in the least bit cool, or shuttered. Her cheeks were tinged with pink. Her eyes looked dark and glittering—an aftermath, no doubt, of the rampant sex they had recently enjoyed. She looked vibrant and delectable.

'More to drink?' she suggested, offering him a frosted can.

He shook his head as he quashed his desire to pull her into his arms, because he always found public declarations of affection faintly distasteful. 'No, thanks.'

She glanced across at him. 'I don't suppose you do this kind of thing very often.'

'Have my offer of a dinner date trashed, you mean?'

A shadow crossed over her face. 'You're not enjoying it?'

Alessio let out a low sigh of frustration. Why were her teeth digging into the soft cushion of her bottom lip like that? He didn't want her to go all uncertain and *cute* on him. He wanted the old Nicola back. The composed, self-possessed woman who kept him a reassuring arm's length away. 'It's different,' he conceded drily. 'I don't think I can ever remember a spontaneous picnic being so heavily dive-bombed by wasps. But thanks for buying me dinner, Nicola. That certainly hasn't happened in a long time.'

She sat back on her heels and plucked a blade of grass from the dusty ground and he got the strangest feeling she was trying not to meet his eyes.

'It must be weird,' she said slowly. 'Being so rich that everyone always expects you to pick up the bill. I suppose you just grow up getting used to it.'

'Or not,' he corrected flatly.

She blinked. 'I don't understand.'

His laugh was tinged with bitterness. 'You think I was born rich?'

'It's a reasonable assumption to make. You're a billionaire.' She ran the blade of grass between two unvarnished fingernails. 'Your family own a vast estate in Tuscany. Your stepfather's an aristocrat. Somehow, I can't imagine you ever having been on the breadline.'

'Well, you're wrong.'

Her lashes shuttered her eyes. 'Am I?'

'Completely.'

She nodded but said nothing more and inexplicably Alessio found himself wanting to talk about it, despite his inbuilt aversion to personal disclosure. Was it his recent brush with the past which had seared it onto the forefront of his mind, along with the knowledge that his mother was refusing to extricate herself from her dysfunctional relationship? Or just that Nicola had fixed her incredible gaze on him, and he wanted to lose himself in the cool, grey depths of those eyes? 'I wasn't born rich,' he said slowly. 'My mother had nothing when I was born. No man and certainly no wedding ring.'

'Your half-sister told me you were illegitimate,' she ventured.

His eyes narrowed. 'But you didn't think to tell me that?'

'Why should I?' She shrugged. 'It was just before dinner and in view of what came next, it sort of slipped my mind. Also, it's none of my business.'

'True. I never even met my father. He was a sailor, according to my mother. She didn't even know his surname.' He gave a bitter laugh. 'Nobody could ever accuse them of being star-crossed lovers.'

But if he had intended to shock her or goad her into passing judgement, she didn't take the bait. In fact, she showed no reaction at all and something about her serenity made him continue.

'We lived hand to mouth.' He closed his eyes and as the evening sun warmed the lids, he took himself back to a very different life—a place he rarely permitted himself to visit. Had he thought that time would lessen its impact? Maybe. But to his surprise, the memory was still sharp. Still vivid. Painfully so. 'We lived with my grandmother in Southern Italy, in a tiny apartment in the mountains. And though we had very little, it was a good life.'

Or so he had thought.

Not so his mother. His beautiful, restless mother. Bitterly resenting the restrictions brought about by childcare, she had left most of the responsibility to his beloved *nonna*. He remembered her endless complaints that her youth was draining away as she regarded their remote, hilltop village with an aggrieved eye. 'I will never find myself a man,' she had moaned, glaring pointedly at her son. 'Not with all this baggage in tow.'

Harsh words for a little boy to hear, but Alessio had been willing to forgive the woman who had given birth to him. At least, in the beginning. Later, it became much harder to forgive.

'My mother felt trapped by her circumstances.' His lashes flickered open and he could see a crowd of tourists outside the gates of Buckingham Palace, their phones held high in the air. 'So she found herself a job as chambermaid in a fancy hotel in Lecce and an escape route, courtesy of a much older man who was staying there. She met an English aristocrat and quickly became pregnant by him.'

'Lord Bonner?' she guessed, and he nodded.

'Edward Bonner,' he agreed. 'It was a huge gamble, because she was running the risk of having two illegitimate children under four. But this time she wasn't deserted, because Edward badly needed an heir. He offered to marry her and take her to England to live in his stately home and begin a new life as Lady Bonner.' He paused. 'I'm sure you don't need me to tell you how delighted she was to be able to escape her life of poverty to become a bona fide member of the aristocracy.'

'But at least she took you with her,' she offered slowly. 'I suppose she could have left you behind.'

'Yes, she took me with her, although that had nothing to do with maternal devotion. I overheard her telling a friend that her refusal to be parted from her son would make her appear more caring to her new husband. At least I was never under any illusions about just how ruthless women could be,' he added harshly.

'So you were brought to England.' Her gaze was steady. 'That must have been quite the upheaval.'

'*Sì.*' He shrugged. 'From two rooms to a Palladian mansion with servants was a pretty big leap for a four-year-old boy.'

He read the empathy in her eyes and now he was beginning to regret having started this. Because knowledge was power and she might be tempted to use it when their brief affair ended. But, despite her expression of distaste when he had handed her the pen, she had signed a confidentiality agreement before travelling out to Umbria, hadn't she? Was it that which made the rest of the story come spilling out, as if he couldn't wait to purge himself of the darkness which had lain within him all these years? How long since he'd allowed himself to think about this? He had been convinced that if you buried unsavoury things deep enough they would rot away, like garbage, but he had been wrong.

He stretched out his legs in front of him. 'When they arrived in England Edward announced there could never be any question of divorce and my mother was delighted because it implied security. The reality was that it gave him carte blanche to behave exactly as he saw fit—and once my half-brother and half-sister were born, my presence in the house became superfluous.' He paused. 'Edward and his legitimate offspring never missed an opportunity to try to make my life a misery.'

'And was that…awful?'

'I'm pretty resilient, Nicola.' He gave a short laugh. 'Let's just say that my admission at seven to one of the most brutal boarding schools in the country came as something of a relief. At least, for a while. I wasn't a natural fit for the English public school system, even though I won the chemistry prize year after year. And despite the entreaties of my tutors, when I was thirteen I announced I was going back to Puglia to live with my grandmother.'

'And your mother didn't try to stop you?'

'Of course she didn't try to stop me,' he said softly. 'I was a constant thorn in my stepfather's side. A powerful reminder of his wife's other lover. There was never any love lost between me and Edward. That party in Tuscany was the first time I've seen them together in years.'

And suddenly it became important for her to understand there had been no handouts along the way. No deeds to expensive houses, or the promise of a large inheritance to cushion every decision he would ever make. 'Everything I've achieved has been through my own endeavours, Nicola. I've done it all on my own. Just a couple of years after I returned to Italy, my grandmother died—'

'Oh, Alessio.'

He didn't want to remember that time. His sense of helplessness and anger as the only woman who had ever really loved him slipped away—ravaged by her disease—had forged his determination that nothing and nobody was ever going to hurt him like that again.

'I knew what she would have wanted and so I worked hard at school and, against all the odds, won a scholarship to Stanford. America gave me the chance to reinvent myself and by the time I'd made my first million, I had paid off every cent my stepfather had ever spent on my education. And I've never looked back.'

He watched as she fiddled with the now-wilted

blade of grass again, before lifting her head to look him full in the face. There were many ways she could have reacted to his story and Alessio was prepared for any of them. She could have bitched about his mother, which would have been unacceptable—because everyone knew it was okay to diss your own mother but nobody else had that right. She could have stated the obvious—that his stepfather was a bastard. What he hadn't been expecting was the quiet compassion shining from those extraordinary eyes. But as their gazes held, her expression changed. The softness in her eyes became edged with the quicksilver gleam of desire. He could see her nipples hardening beneath her white shirt and hunger began to pulse through his veins as he recalled what had happened behind the bronze statue.

'I think we've talked enough, don't you?' He rose to his feet, holding out his hand to assist her, before shaking off the dusty jacket on which she'd been sitting and slinging it over his shoulder. 'My hotel is just across the park,' he said.

And despite her inexperience, Nicola knew exactly what he meant by that careless remark. This was grown-up speak for *let's spend the night together* and she wasn't sure how to respond. Obviously, she wanted to go to bed with him but that mightn't be such a good idea. She was still in her crumpled work clothes for one thing, but that wasn't her main concern. More worrying was the certainty that her feelings were changing. She was starting to care about him, and that had never been on the cards.

She hadn't expected him to open up to her like that. To tell her about his brutal boarding school and the horrible sense of exclusion he had encountered at home, or the break in his voice when he'd talked about his grandmother's death. It was the things he *hadn't* said which had made his story so heartbreaking and it had shown her that nothing was ever as it seemed from the outside. Behind the glittering veneer of the successful billionaire was a man who had been badly damaged. And yet he had trusted her enough to tell her. Didn't that mean something? Were his feelings towards her changing, too?

Excitement rippled over her as she attempted to match his careless tone, because she certainly didn't want to put him off by being too *eager*. But she was. She wanted him so badly it was making her tummy tighten and her breasts were flooding with exquisite heat. 'Okay,' she agreed, pushing her too-hot toes into one of her suede court shoes. 'Though I'm not suitably dressed for a fancy hotel.'

'Who cares about that?' he questioned arrogantly.

They walked the short distance across Green Park to the famous Ritz hotel, where the white-gloved doorman greeted Alessio like an old friend. Inside was an abundance of gleaming marble and lavish flower arrangements and Nicola felt torn as they rode the gleaming elevator, her crumpled clothes making her feel out of place among the well-heeled guests, in their designer silks and diamonds.

But the moment they reached Alessio's suite and he slid his arms around her, she forgot everything. All her worries and insecurities trickled away beneath the seeking power of his kiss. She wondered whether this was going to be like that encounter in the gallery—all hot and raw and urgent—but it couldn't have been more different. His movements were tantalisingly slow as he began to undress her. Almost as if he was determined to demonstrate which of them was in control. But that was a good thing, surely, she figured as his fingertips brushed over her shivering skin.

She closed her eyes as he began to unbutton her shirt, slowly exposing her heated flesh, until she was practically going out of her mind with frustration. Her breasts were pushing hard against a bra which suddenly seemed insubstantial and she gave a gasp as he laved his tongue over her cleavage.

'Mmm...' came his throaty growl of approval as his teeth encountered the delicate lace and she worried that he might rip it. 'Is this some of the lingerie I bought for you?'

It was a question which jarred and Nicola stiffened.

Was he doing his best to remind her that she had been bought and paid for and carried her own particular price tag? Easy come, easy go? Would he have been less aroused if she'd been sporting her usual knickers which were three for the price of two? Perhaps if he hadn't chosen that precise moment to unclip the catch of her bra, she might have objected and pushed him away, but her aching breasts had now slipped free and he had captured them in his palms. And…

A shuddered sigh left her lungs. Sweet heaven. Who *cared* about who had bought her underwear? All she could think about was Alessio sucking on one nipple, while removing her panties. And then he was touching her just as he'd done before. Feathering his finger against her honeyed heat until she was coming apart, her knees buckling and her body bucking as he brought her to another swift climax.

The bed on which he placed her was enormous but all Nicola could think about was that, once again, Alessio's control seemed to have vanished—for he was tearing off his shirt with little regard for its fate. He was slightly more considered when unzipping his trousers and Nicola shut her eyes as the hard length of his arousal was revealed, suddenly self-conscious.

Because this wasn't like when they'd been in Italy and had come together like two strangers. Now she knew him better and somehow that made intimacy slightly more awkward. It was harder not to *care* about him, yet she didn't want to scare him off by revealing that. She wanted to grasp the familiar mantle of neutrality, but somehow it was eluding her. Was this what happened when a man started to invade your heart and your body—that your sense of self seemed to slip away?

'Look at me, *cara*,' he urged.

Reluctantly, she opened her eyes.

'Don't ever be inhibited around your lovers, Nicola,' he purred. 'Men enjoy seeing a woman gaze at them. They like to watch their eyes darken with desire.' His gaze was slitted with gleamed approval. 'Just as yours are doing now.'

It was no hardship to study his honed and golden flesh, but as she drank in his raw, masculine beauty Nicola was filled with confusion, his words sowing seeds of doubt in a mind which had always been a fertile breeding ground for rejection. Why was he talking about her *lovers* like that—when he was the only lover she'd ever had?

The only one she could ever imagine wanting.

But there was no time to dwell on her fears because soon he had her moaning again as he filled her with his hardness.

His movements were deep and the confident thrust of her pelvis made him utter something helpless in Italian. And when she could hold back no longer, she began to spasm around him as he shuddered out his own fulfilment. And didn't that shared moment of orgasm feel extra special? Was that *tenderness* she could feel in his kiss? Was it that which made a rush of longing swell up inside her and stupid tears prick the backs of her eyes, so that she had to blink them away and turn her head away, praying he hadn't noticed?

The room was quiet and, with a lazy yawn, Alessio gazed out of the window at the green blur of leaves in the treetops. It felt good to look at nature for a change, he reflected, after years of the metal and glass view of his high-tech Manhattan penthouse. He stretched, unable to shake off this exquisite sense of lethargy as he tried get his head around what had just happened. The sex had been unbelievable, *sì*. In fact, he would go so far as to admit it was the best sex he'd ever had, which was saying something, given his extensive track record. But just before that last incredible orgasm, he had heard something which had hovered disturbingly on the edges of his mind and was coming back to him now with unwelcome clarity. Had that been a muffled sob choking from Nicola's lips? The telltale sound of unwanted emotion intruding?

He frowned because their chemistry was off the scale, *sì*, but was purely physical. He knew that and she needed to know it, too. Before she started to care. Before she fell in love with him, as so many others had done, even though he'd never given anyone cause to love him. Women like his mother, for whom a man's wealth was paramount. Women who would sacrifice a child's happiness as a means to an end.

But Nicola was different from other women, he

conceded. And not just because she had chosen a sandwich in the park—which she had paid for—instead of eating in a luxury restaurant. He recognised that in many ways she was still an innocent and he respected her too much to break her heart. Turning over, he reached for her—the tantalising throb of an erection making him regret the inevitability of what he was about to say.

'You know I have to fly to Japan tomorrow?'

'I don't think you mentioned it, no.' That polite, gallery smile was back. 'I'm sure it will be lovely. Although I've never been there, of course.'

He frowned, because he had been expecting *some* sort of disappointment, not that shrugging acceptance. 'I was thinking that next time I'm in London—' he kept his voice deliberately casual '—we could see each other.'

Her wary expression didn't change. 'Sure. Why not?'

Her lips were so inviting that he might have left the subject alone and kissed her into sweet oblivion if he hadn't noticed the shiny streak of a dried tear on her cheek, which was enough to reinforce his resolve. Because if this was to continue in the way he intended it to, it was vital that he set down some rules, right from the start.

'I like you, Nicola,' he said slowly. 'In fact, I like you a lot. You're bright and funny and beautiful and one day you're going to meet an amazing man and marry him.' He paused as he met the question in her eyes. 'But that man isn't going to be me.'

He waited for the inevitable storm. For fireworks and indignation. But there were none. That serene mask was back in place and, ironically, he wanted to shatter it—to glimpse the passion she only ever showed when he was deep inside her. But there was no passion on her face now. Just cool calculation.

'The first time I had dinner with you,' she said calmly, as if they were discussing nothing more controversial than the sandwich they had eaten in the park, 'I told you that I didn't want to marry anyone. Which remains true. I also remember saying, very explicitly, that even if I did—*even if I did*—you would be the last person on earth I would ever choose. Which also happened to be true. And my position on that hasn't changed.'

She flicked a thick handful of blonde hair over her bare shoulder. 'So I find it more than a little irritating to have been cast in the role of some sort of pining desperado—no, please don't interrupt me, Alessio—which seems more about feeding *your* ego than reflecting *my* feelings with any degree of accuracy.'

Taken aback by her objections and more than a little aroused by her cool logic and, of course, by the provocative movement of her breasts, Alessio held up his palms in a gesture of mock submission. '*Bene, bene!* You've convinced me. I just wanted to put it out there, that's all. So that there could be no misunderstanding.'

There was a pause and her eyes glinted with what might have been humour, but it might have been something else. Something both dangerous and alluring.

'You seem to be the only one in danger of misunderstanding, if you don't mind my saying so.'

He frowned. Would she consider it patronising if he admitted that it had been an unexpected feeling of *protectiveness* which had inspired his words to her? A desire not to hurt her, rather than a desire to feed his ego. He suspected she would. He met her shuttered grey stare. 'I still want you,' he said simply.

Nicola could see that for herself. The unmistakable outline of his erection was visible beneath the fine linen sheet and that realisation provoked an answering stab of heat, low in her sex. She could feel her breasts begin to flood and from the quick flicker of his sapphire gaze, she could tell that her reaction hadn't escaped him.

What would most women in this situation do? she wondered desperately. She supposed it depended on what they wanted. If they were holding out for commitment, then they might just cut their losses and leave. It would hurt for a while, but they'd get over it.

But she wasn't holding out for commitment.

She had lost her virginity to him. The only thing she had left to lose was her heart and that didn't *have* to happen—not as long as she guarded it fiercely. Because here was an opportunity to learn. The same kind of opportunity which had propelled her from abject poverty into one of the plushest art galleries in Mayfair. She had become an expert and, likewise, could learn from Alessio by watching and listening and, of course, participating. But this wouldn't involve studying by torchlight while everyone else was asleep, or juggling two waitress jobs while she studied hard at night school. This would consist of lessons in sex from someone who was unbelievably good at it.

'And I want you, too. Isn't that why I'm here?' But it still took a lot of nerve to actually come out and say it. 'Because you can teach me.'

He frowned. 'Teach you what?'

'Everything you know.' She shrugged. 'About sex.'

His eyes narrowed. 'You're not making any sense.'

'Think about it, Alessio,' she challenged softly. 'You're experienced and I'm not—but I've always been an excellent student.' The perplexed darkening of his blue eyes gave her a sudden heady rush of satisfaction, because this was a Nicola she felt comfortable with. Who saw what she wanted and went out to get it. 'And obviously—given my rather competitive nature—I want to be the best lover I can. And you can show me how to achieve that.' She paused. 'Can't you?'

His face was a picture. There was desire—yes, but it was the flicker of uncertainty in his eyes that made him seem more human. More accessible. And that was dangerous. She couldn't possibly make such a cold-blooded demand if she was then going to commit the cardinal crime of falling in love with him. There was no point in being bold and ambitious if she then came over as vulnerable.

But he had recovered his equilibrium and his faint consternation had been replaced by a slow smile of anticipation which was making her tummy tighten. 'You want me to teach you everything I know about sex, do you, *cara*?' he murmured, sliding his hand between her thighs to target her aching bud. 'It's certainly the most unconventional request I've ever received from a woman but rest assured, Nicola, it will be my pleasure. And yours, of course.'

'Oh!' she said faintly as he began to strum her aroused flesh and before too long she was contracting around his finger and choking out his name. As powerful waves of pleasure washed over her she pulled his head towards hers and her last thought before their lips met was that she could handle this.

Of course she could.

CHAPTER ELEVEN

THE WIND WAS biting as Alessio emerged from his Munich flight and slid into the limousine waiting on the runway, ready to speed him towards central London. Lost in thought, he stared out of the window, barely registering the red-gold blur of autumn leaves swirling through the air. But for once he wasn't preoccupied with his latest project, nor the rapid global expansion of his chemical company, which had made him the wunderkind of the international markets.

No, his mind was consumed with one thing, and one thing only. His mouth grew dry. A woman with glacial eyes and a pale fall of hair, with an irritating habit of failing to return his calls.

Nicola.

Tantalising, aloof Nicola Bennett, who was driving him completely crazy.

He scowled.

He had imagined that her elusiveness might have dissolved a little by now, but he had been wrong. Her behaviour still perplexed him and he couldn't shake off the sense that, somehow, she was running rings around him. He wondered if she had any idea just how much he'd gone out of his way to accommodate her wishes. She wanted him to teach her about sex? Fine. He was more than happy to oblige. A muscle fired at his temple. Which meant there had to be a little give and take, since they lived on opposite sides of the globe.

What was so wrong with diverting his flight last week and ringing her unexpectedly at midnight? He had suggested she get over to his hotel as quickly as possible, promising that he'd be able to devote most of the following day to her, before returning to Manhattan. But her anticipated delight hadn't been forthcoming—and neither had his fantasy that she would arrive shortly afterwards, wearing very little underneath her coat. Instead, he had been subjected to an uncomfortable barrage of questions.

Was it too much to ask that he give her some notice? she had demanded coolly. Or was she just expected to cancel her existing plans in order to see him?

He had replied—with equal cool—that he didn't *expect* her to do anything and she should only cancel her plans if she wanted to see him, which it appeared she didn't. Because she had turned him down flat and told him to contact her next time he was in London! At first, he had been disbelieving, then angry and then—bizarrely—curiously chastened. It had made him re-evaluate the way he treated women and think that maybe she deserved better. It had occurred to him that he might have to start doing things differently with her—but this realisation was cushioned by the reassuring rider that it wouldn't impact too significantly on his life. Because there was no perceived threat from Nicola Bennett. Their agreement had been straightforward from the start—a basic sexual compatibility which wasn't complicated by unrealistic emotional demands.

Which was why he had given her plenty of warning before arranging to meet her for dinner tonight. He'd offered to rebook the Starlight Room at the Granchester—the no-show destination of their first date—but to his surprise she had said it was too public and couldn't he find somewhere more discreet?

No, she definitely wasn't like other women.

Perhaps it was time he got to know her a little better. Would that lessen his fascination for her, he wondered idly—or simply increase it?

He leaned back against the leather seat and gave a soft sigh of satisfaction, because never before could he recall feeling such a heightened degree of anticipation.

Nicola flipped the door sign to *Closed* and turned to find Sergio watching her.

'Is everything okay?' he asked.

Nicola smiled at her boss, trying to reclaim the familiar sense of calm which seemed to have been eluding her these past few weeks—but it wasn't easy. Not when Sergio was hovering right beside the spot where she'd enjoyed that hot encounter with Alessio last month. Were they *ever* going to sell that wretched bronze—or was she doomed to endure a daily reminder of how decadent she had been?

'I'm fine, thank you, Sergio,' she answered politely, but didn't pursue the conversation. She didn't want to give him any opportunity to probe, but it seemed that, for once, his curiosity was roused.

'It's just that you seem…' He shrugged. 'It's hard to put into words.'

'Then don't even try!' Her words were bright. 'After all, I've sold three paintings this week, haven't I?'

'This is true, you have. With two more in the pipeline. Nobody could ever question your commitment or your success, Nicola. You just seem different, that's all.' He narrowed his eyes. 'Distracted.'

'Maybe it's the autumn weather. Chill in the air and all that. Look, I'd better get on. I've still got an email I need to send before I can go home.'

But there was truth in his words and she wondered what Sergio would say if she told him *why* she was so distracted. If she just happened to explain that she was conducting a clandestine relationship with one of his oldest friends and trying very hard to keep her feelings compartmentalised—a task being severely compromised by a lack of sleep and the constant gnaw of worry. Because Stacey had given birth three short weeks ago and the new mother was finding it a struggle. Actually, that was an understatement.

It had been a difficult birth and Nicola was discovering that nothing could really prepare you for the arrival of a screaming newborn. Little Jago was tiny and unbelievably cute, but solo parenthood was always going to be a challenge and nobody could take away the painful fact that his daddy was in prison—though Nicola had done her best to compensate for her brother's absence.

Some nights she'd slept on the floor of Stacey's living room, getting up to feed the baby to give the new mum a chance to rest. And of course, on nights when Alessio was in town, she got practically no sleep at all, though for very different reasons. But these late nights and early mornings were beginning to show. She'd used an inordinate amount of foundation on her face—but even the smooth matte finish couldn't disguise the inky shadows beneath her eyes.

Yet, despite the massive worry brought about by the birth of her new nephew, at times Nicola had felt almost *high* with happiness. Sometimes she wondered if it was wrong to enjoy such a giddy sense of well-being when Stacey was finding it so difficult to cope. But she couldn't help herself, no matter how much she tried to temper her feelings, or force herself to refuse Alessio's last-minute invite last week, because at the time she'd been dealing with dirty nappies. Bottom line—no pun intended—ever since she'd asked the billionaire chemist to teach her about sex, she'd been seeing him whenever he was in London. And every time she did, it just got better.

She felt the hard clench of her heart. Not just physically. That was the trouble. Everything about their affair was good. All the things she'd tried not to dream of were hers for the taking, because Alessio di Bari was an amazing man. Generous, intelligent and sexy—with a dry wit which often took her by surprise. Sometimes she wondered if he seemed so relaxed in her company because she'd been so adamant about not wanting a permanent relationship. Or did it all boil down to their insane chemistry—his specialist subject, as it happened—which combusted whenever they came close?

She glanced at her watch, realising there was no time to waste on unanswerable questions. She needed to hurry so she would be ready in time to meet him. In the end it was all a bit of a rush—especially as she went home via Stacey's apartment, although she was still wearing her work clothes, which meant that, because Jago was full of cold, he covered her jacket in snot before giving another angry squall.

'He never stops!' wailed Stacey.

'Shh… Shh…' Nicola cradled the tiny baby and smoothed damp, wispy curls away from his forehead. 'Don't worry. He won't be like this for ever—and he's just got a bit of a cold, hasn't he? It's always difficult at the beginning, Stace. All the books say that.'

Stacey nodded, but her lips were working frantically as if she was trying very hard not to cry. Nicola's heart went out to the new mother as she made her a pot of tea and a sandwich, before rushing off home to get ready. Trying to fight off the plastic flap of the shower curtain, which kept sticking to her skin, she wondered what kind of future there would be for little Jago, with a father who was in and out of jail and a young couple with practically no prospects.

But *she* had done it, hadn't she? *She* had climbed out of the gutter and made something of herself without help from anyone else. And she would be around for Jago. Free of any family demands of her own and probably earning loads more money by then—there was no reason why she couldn't become a guiding presence in his life.

Her phone pinged, her heart giving a predictable leap when she read the message.

Where are you?

She replied, trying to emulate his terse style.

On my way.

She had requested a venue less public than the Starlight Room because she didn't want word getting back to Sergio on the grapevine—but the moment she walked into the restaurant Alessio had chosen as an alternative, she wished she'd kept her mouth shut. Because this was very private, yes—achingly so. Worse still, it was romantic. The flicker of tall creamy candles was the predominant source of lighting and it gave the room an intensely intimate feel. Rich brocade fabric lined the walls and there were heavy velvet drapes in darkly jewelled shades of emerald and crimson. It made her think of things she had no right to be thinking—about love and longevity and what was going to happen to them. About how much longer she could maintain this façade of not caring for him.

Alessio was rising to his feet, just as he'd done the first time they'd had dinner together. But things had changed. Back then she had been wary of him and he had been wary, too. She remembered the faint air of hostility which had radiated from his brooding frame. There had been calculating appraisal—from both of them—not this extended eye contact which managed to convey a wealth of repressed longing in a single moment. But nothing *had* changed, Nicola reminded herself fiercely. Not really. Only her own stupid mindset. *She* was the one who had started romanticising about what was only ever intended to be a functional relationship.

'Hi,' she said as she slid into her seat, slightly inhibited by the narrow skirt of her apricot silk dress. 'Hope I haven't kept you waiting.'

'Well, you have—but I thought that was your modus operandi,' he offered drily.

'I'm a busy working woman,' she returned, with a smile. 'How's life in Manhattan?'

'I've barely been there all month. Stockholm. Geneva. Munich.'

'That sounds like remarkably little down-time to me.'

'Isn't that what I'm doing right now?' He paused, his blue eyes slanting her a look of soft promise. 'How's life in London?'

'Oh, you know. Same old, same old.' Sitting back while the waiter filled their flutes with champagne, she wondered what he'd say if she told him she'd been acting as a quasi-mother since she'd last seen him. That the woman in the sleek apricot dress had been sponging the shoulder of her work shirt just an hour earlier. 'Are we celebrating something?' she questioned, watching as straw-coloured foam fizzed up the side of her glass.

'We could be.' He shrugged and smiled. 'The German branch of my company has turned in record profits for the first half of the year.'

'And does that…does something like that give you an inordinate amount of pleasure?'

'No, Nicola.' There was a pause. '*You* give me an inordinate amount of pleasure.'

Nicola's heart thudded, because when he looked at her that way—with that smoky expression which made his blue eyes smoulder—it made her feel dizzy with desire. It's sex, she reminded herself weakly. And because that's *all* it is, you need to showcase some of your newly learned expertise. He doesn't want a lover who's going to gaze at him with her mouth open like a stranded fish, while imagining what his first-born might look like. He wants a sassy woman who's going to turn him on.

'Is this going to turn into some sort of verbal foreplay?' she questioned quietly. 'Are you going to make me want you so much that I won't be able to concentrate on what I'm eating?'

'On the contrary,' he demurred silkily. 'I intend to feed every one of your senses tonight, Nicola. And also—' He halted as the head waiter arrived at their table, obviously keen to discuss the merits of the menu and wine list, but Alessio simply raised his eyebrows at Nicola. 'Shall I order?'

She nodded and waited until the waiter had gone away before looking at him quizzically. 'You were saying?'

What *had* he been saying? Alessio frowned. It was difficult to recall a word, let alone a sentence, when she was dazzling him with all her fresh blonde beauty, which he had missed during the fortnight they'd been apart. When she had arrived here tonight, every man had turned to watch her but she had been totally oblivious. She had no idea just how alluring she was and he liked that about her, he realised suddenly.

'I've been thinking—'

'Oh, dear. Could be dangerous.'

'It suddenly occurred to me how much I've told you about myself,' he mused. 'Things I've never told anyone else.'

A sudden tension had crept into her shoulders, which was at odds with the lightness of her response. 'And should I be flattered?'

'That's up to you.' He put his glass down and studied her. 'But since the balance of information between us is so unevenly distributed, don't you think it's time we did something to redress that?'

Nicola couldn't compute his words and not just because he was talking in that analytical and scientific way of his. In fact, she was having difficulty catching her breath, because wasn't this what she had been secretly dreading for weeks? She might have limited experience of dating men, but she wasn't stupid. She'd been aware for a while that Alessio was relaxing his guard more and more, and that a closeness between them seemed to be developing. At first she'd put it down to sex until she was forced to acknowledge that they shared a compatibility outside bed, which she suspected was rare for him. But she had wanted things to stay exactly as they were, because it was safer that way. To preserve their transatlantic affair in aspic and keep it perfect. *This* had never been on her agenda. He wasn't *supposed* to want to get to know her better.

Like all men, he hadn't been interested in asking her any personal questions and she had been more than content for that state of affairs to continue. Hoping her smile didn't betray her sudden nerves, she tilted her head to one side. 'And how do you propose we go about that?'

'Oh, come, Nicola. It's not rocket science.'

'No, because I guess that would be your speciality.'

His eyes glittered. 'Just tell me something about your life.'

'My life?' she echoed weakly. 'Like what?'

'Parents. Siblings. Where you were born. Whether your mother used to bake you a cake for your birthday—that kind of thing. That's not such a big ask, is it?' He ran his finger around the edge of his crystal goblet. 'I thought all women liked to talk about themselves.'

Nicola plucked a bread roll from the basket on the table and proceeded to crumble it into a small pile of crumbs on her side plate. And all the time her mind was performing somersaults. She thought about what she could tell him about her growing-up years. Her

mother baking a cake! It might have been funny if
it weren't so sad.

Because even if Alessio were somebody ordinary—if he'd grown up in the suburbs, eating a roast
dinner every Sunday—her story would still ruffle
the feathers of all but the most liberal-minded. And
Alessio was definitely *not* ordinary. Far from it. He
wasn't asking because he *cared* about her, but because the distribution of information was unequal
and he was a scientist who liked a sense of balance.
What if she blurted out the truth about the current situation with Stacey and baby Jago? If she mentioned
that she didn't know what would happen once Callum was released. Mightn't he respond in the same
way he had done last time, with that slightly arrogant
smile curving his lips as he reached for his meta-
phorical wallet?

'How much do you need?'

That would be unendurable.

Last time he'd offered her money, it had been
nothing but a transaction. He had needed something from her and had paid for it accordingly. But
now it was different. She was having sex with him.
How would she feel if he offered her money now?
Her skin grew icy. Like her mother? The mother she
had vowed never to emulate, who would take whatever she could from a man in return for 'favours'.
She stared down at the crumbled bread, knowing
she had a choice. She could refuse to answer him,

but she suspected that would create even more problems. Or she could shut the conversation down right now, leave—and never see him again. He was certainly too proud to demand to know why she had walked away.

But that was an over-the-top response because she didn't want to walk away. Not yet. Not when he was still giving her the kind of pleasure she'd never thought could exist for someone like her. It would end soon enough. So why not satisfy his curiosity and give him a *version* of her life? Because wasn't that what everyone did, when it boiled down to it? They edited their backstory to make it palatable.

'I was born in East London and, like you, I didn't ever get to meet my father. So, well… I'm illegitimate, too.'

He nodded as he absorbed this, but he didn't comment on it. 'And your mother?'

'She's still alive.'

'You still see her?'

'Of course. Not that often.'

'And brothers? Sisters?'

'I have one brother. He's…he's away a lot of the time.' Nicola knew she was playing with words, but what was the alternative? Ill-disguised horror as she exposed the brittle roots of the Bennett family tree? No. She wanted to keep this as brief as possible. 'His girlfriend Stacey has just had a baby.'

She chose that last statement deliberately, knowing his aversion to having children, but to her surprise, he smiled.

'So you're an aunt?'

'Yes, I'm an aunt.'

'Boy or girl?'

'A little boy. Jago.'

'Ah. His father must be pleased.'

She wanted to tell him to stop being so unpredictable. Why was he reacting with consideration on a subject which couldn't possibly interest him? Because it was confusing the hell out of her. When he was tearing off her clothes she knew exactly where she stood, but right now he was sending out mixed messages and she was terrified of getting the wrong idea. His brow was creased in a faint frown, as if her brief replies weren't what he had been expecting—but fortunately their oysters arrived and fussing with lemon quarters and raspberry vinegar gave her time to compose herself.

'Mmm...' she said, but even though she usually loved oysters, the cold mollusc felt faintly repugnant as it slid down her throat. Suddenly she heard her phone vibrating from the bottom of her handbag and some sixth sense urged her not to ignore it, because who would ring her at this time of night unless something was wrong? Knowing she was about to break a social taboo, she met Alessio's gaze across the table. 'Would you mind if I answered that?'

His sapphire eyes grew shuttered. 'Must you?'

But Nicola was already pulling the phone from her handbag, her skin growing clammy as a picture of Jago flashed up and she saw the alert at the top of the screen. Four missed calls from Stacey.

'I've got to answer this,' she blurted out, rising to her feet and stumbling from the room, barely aware of the waiter she almost cannoned into, who narrowly avoided dropping a tray of cocktails. But the call had ended by the time she reached the restaurant foyer and when Nicola jabbed the 'return call' button, Stacey picked up immediately, her voice incomprehensible through the sound of Jago crying in the background.

'What's happening?' Nicola sucked in a breath. 'Is Jago okay?'

'I'm a bit worried, Nic. He's breathing a bit fast and won't take his bottle, and he's—'

Her words were interrupted by a snuffly wail and Nicola thought very quickly. It could be something or it could be nothing, but was it really a risk worth taking? And didn't Stacey need all the support she could get right now? 'I'm coming over,' she said. 'If you're really worried then call an ambulance, but if I jump in a cab I can be there in twenty minutes.'

'I'll wait,' said Stacey, her voice filled with gratitude.

With trembling fingers Nicola cut the connection and looked up to see Alessio standing in front of her in the restaurant foyer, his face shadowed and grave.

'I have to go!'

'I heard. My car will take you. You can tell me what's happening on the way.'

Nicola opened her mouth then shut it again as his car pulled up outside the restaurant, because only a fool would refuse his offer of assistance. All the barriers she had previously erected to keep him out of her life seemed irrelevant now as she nodded her head. Stumbling out the address, she was barely aware of the limousine door slamming shut, or the speed at which Alessio's chauffeur negotiated London's narrow side streets.

'Are you going to tell me what's going on?' Alessio demanded urgently.

'Jago won't take his bottle.' Nervously, her fingers played with the thin gold chain at her neck. 'He's all snuffly and I can tell Stacey's worried. If she needs to take him to hospital, it's much better if she has someone with her.'

He frowned. 'Isn't your brother with her?'

'No. My brother...' And suddenly the words just came blurting out. 'My brother's in jail!' She saw his lips flatten as he took out his phone and began punching out a number. 'What are you doing?'

'Calling a friend who's a paediatrician.'

'I don't—'

Imperiously holding up his hand for silence, he began to speak but Nicola barely registered a word he said, she was just wishing they would get there. Before too long the car was drawing up outside the flat and she was running upstairs and Stacey was letting her in, the baby cradled against one shoulder.

'Here. Let's put him on the sofa and have a look at him,' said Nicola.

She laid him down carefully, her heart contracting as she observed the rapid rise and fall of his tiny chest, and she was just about to phone an ambulance when the door opened and Alessio walked in, accompanied by a tall and incredibly good-looking man wearing motorcycle leathers and carrying a bag.

'What's going on?' demanded Stacey. 'Who are you?'

'I'm Alessio di Bari, a friend of Nicola's, and this is Harrison Drake, a friend of *mine* and one of the finest paediatricians in the country.'

At this, Stacey began to tremble. 'Just help my baby, will you? Please.' The urgency of her plea plunged the room into silence save for the sound of little Jago's breathing as the doctor began to examine him.

Nicola watched as Harrison gently unbuttoned the infant's sleepsuit and listened to his chest with a stethoscope, all the while directing a stream of questions at Stacey. At last, he straightened up, and nodded.

'He's got a mild dose of bronchiolitis, which is very common in young babies. You need to monitor him throughout the night and make sure you feed him less, but more often. I've got some nasal saline drops in my bag—you can give him those and they should help. If his breathing gets faster or more laboured then you should take him to hospital, but I think he's going to be fine.'

Close to tears, Stacey thanked the paediatrician and Nicola realised that sometimes just the positive words of a healthcare professional could be enough to reassure you when you were young and inexperienced. She helped Stacey prepare a bottle for Jago, dimly aware of Alessio leaving the tiny apartment to accompany the doctor downstairs and it came almost as a shock when he returned. Had she thought that would be the last she ever saw of him? That he'd be frightened off by all the chaos and the poverty he had witnessed? Yes, she had. He stood silently in the doorway as she cradled her tiny nephew and suddenly she felt acutely self-conscious about the way he was watching her.

'Thanks for that,' she said at last, laying the now-sleeping baby into his cot and straightening up. 'Your friend was brilliant.'

She wondered if he'd heard her because he didn't reply but then she realised he was looking round the apartment. And suddenly Nicola saw it through his eyes. The open pack of disposable nappies next to the TV, and the line of tiny sleepsuits drying on the radiator. Three dirty cups were sitting on the paper-strewn coffee table, along with the remains of a cheese sandwich. Why was Stacey so *untidy*? she found herself thinking.

He turned then and Nicola almost recoiled from the expression on his face, because Alessio had never looked at her like this before, not even at the beginning. His features looked as if they had been carved from some obsidian marble and his blue eyes were shuttered and cold. He was only on the other side of the small room, but he seemed so far away that he might have been on another planet. Was he *judging* them?

'I'm going to stay here with Jago and Stacey tonight,' she said, offering an explanation he hadn't asked for.

Afterwards she wondered what she'd been hoping he'd say. That he would see her tomorrow, as planned? Place his hand on her arm in a gesture of comfort, or even give her a hug? But he didn't. He remained exactly where he was—as if her proximity might contaminate him in some way.

But his features softened a little as he turned to Stacey and his deep voice was immensely kind—and something about both those things filled Nicola with a sense of wistfulness, which made her heart contract with hopeless longing.

'Goodnight, Stacey,' he said quietly. 'Take heart from Harrison's words, and, in the meantime, I will say a prayer for your son.'

CHAPTER TWELVE

FENDING OFF QUESTIONS about the identity of their knight in shining armour, Nicola took the following week off work and moved in to help Stacey with Jago, who delighted them all with his rapid and robust recovery. It was good to be able to offer support she thought, and—importantly—it kept her busy.

She managed to track down Harrison Drake's address to discover he was a consultant at London's biggest paediatric hospital and sent a thank you card, as well as a contribution to his research project. She also attempted to demonstrate to Stacey the benefits of keeping a small space tidy and was surprised by the success of her endeavours—she'd certainly never seen the place look so neat before, nor the fridge stocked with so much healthy food. Her brother's girlfriend had even started talking about learning how to cook. Maybe Jago's sickness had been the wake-up call she'd needed. As if she'd suddenly realised she needed to make life as good as it possibly could be for her tiny baby and for Callum, when he was eventually released.

But no matter how many questions Stacey asked about Alessio, Nicola blocked them all.

She didn't want to talk about him.

She didn't even want to think about him.

Some hope.

He was constantly on her mind. When she was making coffee in the morning, or forcing herself to eat a salad from the deli at lunchtime. In the bath, and in her dreams. Especially her dreams. Perhaps it was true what they said about absence making the heart grow fonder and that was the reason he was obsessing her thoughts so much. Because Nicola hadn't heard from Alessio since the night of Jago's illness— not a single word—and that had left her feeling hurt and bewildered. Was it over? Just like that? She'd known the relationship was always destined to end and there was never going to be an easy way for that to happen, but this felt unsatisfactory. Unfinished.

She remembered his cold and forbidding expression as he had surveyed her from the other side of the room. His failure to reach out and comfort her. Had he been appalled by that unexpected glimpse into the chaos of her private life? Had it driven home her complete unsuitability to be the lover of a man like him? Several times she picked up the phone to text him, but never followed through, aware that falsely cheerful messages were never convincing and ran the risk of making her look desperate.

But she knew from past experience that the only way to move forward was to learn from the past and grab at the present with both hands. It was pointless wondering why she had been ghosted from Alessio's life. It hurt more than she had ever imagined it would—but she would get over it.

She threw herself into promoting the gallery's latest collection of seascapes by an artist from South Devon, which had opened to great fanfare in the art world. She took a trip to Northumbria to advise on the hanging of a collection of paintings in a private home. Yet, despite all her best intentions, the days all seemed to bleed into each other until one was indistinguishable from the next. The autumn winds were fierce, the bronze statue *still* hadn't sold and the shorter, colder days filled Nicola with a gloom which wouldn't seem to shift.

In an attempt to shake herself out of her lethargy, she went hiking one Sunday morning, bought a newspaper on the way back and had just settled down to read it when the shrill ring of the doorbell disturbed her. Putting down the paper, she frowned. Because she hadn't invited anyone round. In truth, she never did. Old habits died hard. This was *her* space. Her refuge. It was small, yes, but it was all hers—so long as she kept paying the rent—and she felt safe here.

But when she peered into the door viewer, she froze. Shock iced over her skin, her heart squeezing painfully in her chest when she saw who was standing there. Tall, dark and indescribably sexy. The man who had been haunting her sleeping and her waking hours. Leaning against the wall for support, she closed her eyes and fought to control her rapid breathing.

Alessio.

Here.

She swallowed. Now what?

The Nicola she had been when she'd first met him would have quizzed him coolly over the intercom, but the Nicola she had become was aching to see him again…unable to stop her imagination from going into fantasy overdrive as she buzzed him in. But the moment she opened the door she realised just how stupid that fantasy had been. Alessio wasn't here because he had missed her, or because he wanted her—at least, not if his grim expression was anything to go by.

'How's Jago?' he demanded.

'Better,' she said, touched by his solicitude and softening a little. 'Completely better, actually. I… I probably should have let you know.'

'Yes, you probably should—although I gather you sent a note to Harrison,' he said, shooting her a blue bullet of a stare. 'Are you going to let me in, Nicola?'

he questioned, with quiet, scientific precision. 'Or are you still intent on keeping me out of your home?'

'Of course,' she said, opening the door wider.

He stepped inside and, in a funny sort of way, the continued flintiness of his expression helped bring Nicola to her senses. Time to cancel the fairy tale, she realised. Time to let go of the dream. 'How *did* you find out where I lived?' she asked dully.

'I got your address from Sergio.'

She stared at him in dismay. 'You didn't tell him—?'

'That we've been having sex?' He gave a short laugh. 'No, I didn't tell him. Don't worry, Nicola. Your ice-maiden status remains intact. He may have been curious but I certainly didn't enlighten him by explaining that up until recently I had been fulfilling a position as your occasional *stud.*' His mouth twisted. 'Good enough to sleep with but not good enough to share any other parts of your life.'

His abrasive words indicated the true depth of his hostility and Nicola wondered if it had always been there, simmering beneath the surface. She could feel herself slowly deflating, like a helium balloon being speared by a pin, and knew she couldn't allow that to happen. She had to be strong, because strength was about the only thing she had left. That, and her pride. 'Why are you here, Alessio?' she said quietly.

He nodded, as if he had been expecting this question a lot sooner, fingers dipping into his jacket pocket before withdrawing something which glittered like a coiled serpent in the centre of his palm. A modestly thin gold chain. Her only piece of 'real' jewellery and something she'd saved up for—fulfilling a stupid desire to fit in with the sophisticated world she sometimes inhabited. She blinked at it before looking up. 'I was wondering where that was,' she said, but couldn't deny the great stab of disappointment which speared her heart as she met his sapphire gaze. He'd come to return her necklace and that was the reason he was here. The only reason. Of course it was.

She took it from him gingerly and put it down on the nearest flat surface, knowing that she had to get rid of him before she did something stupid. Like breaking down, or begging him to pull her into his arms and kiss away her heartache and her aching sense of loneliness. 'Is there anything else?' she enquired coolly.

'Actually, there is. I'm curious and perhaps you can assuage my curiosity. I assume that the money I paid you was used to help your brother and his family—because I sure as hell can't see any of the new furniture you claimed to need.' His gaze flicked over her. 'I mean, why all the mystery, Nicola? The evasion and obfuscation? The double life you appear to have been leading…the brother who's actually in prison, not "away" as you euphemistically put it?'

She shook her head, stupidly wishing she'd had a

chance to brush her hair. But it was pointless wanting his eyes to grow warm with desire or affection, because that ship had clearly sailed. Suddenly this became about defending her position. About battling for some kind of recognition and respect, as she'd done so many times before.

'You want to know *why*?' she demanded, her protective cloak of calm slipping away from her. 'You think I was ashamed of my past?' She nodded. 'Well, yes. Maybe some small part of me *was* ashamed and maybe you would have been, too, if you were me. Because while we were both born illegitimate, our circumstances couldn't have been more different. Oh, don't worry—I'm not trying to raise you on the poverty stakes. But the fact is I grew up in a *slum*, Alessio—with a mother who lived a very dodgy life. She went missing for long periods and we never knew where. My little brother and I were always cold and never had enough to eat and…' Her voice grew a little shaky as the harsh reality of those days came rushing back. 'Whatever food we had, I always gave to Callum, and sometimes I used to steal my classmates' sandwiches for myself, if I thought I could get away with it. There!' She looked at him defiantly. 'Are you shocked?'

But his stony features showed no reaction. 'Go on.'

Nicola sucked in another breath. She'd bottled this up for so long it was as if someone had suddenly shaken that bottle, so that all the words were pouring out. 'Most of my energy was spent battling the social services who wanted to take us into care. They threatened to split us up and I was never going to allow that to happen. Maybe I should have done,' she added bitterly. 'And then Callum wouldn't have ended up getting in with a bad crowd and forging a useless career as a thief. Or maybe I set him a bad example by nicking those sandwiches.' She walked to the other side of the room, hoping the movement would divert his attention from the fact that she was trembling.

'I had to fight for everything I've achieved,' she continued huskily. 'And I've done it by leaving that girl far behind. I had to learn to fit in with the new world I inhabited and was always terrified someone was going to find me out, and judge me. It was a bad case of imposter syndrome. That's why I felt safe here, in my own little place, because I'd never had that before. And okay—I never invited you round before, but you weren't exactly begging me to visit you in Manhattan, were you, Alessio? Our two worlds were never supposed to have met, let alone blended.' She stared at him, unable to keep the sudden flare of hope from her heart. '*Now* do you understand why I didn't tell you?'

But he shook his head—his expression stubborn and intractable. 'I would have preferred to have known the truth, no matter how unpalatable,' he said coldly. 'Remember, I told you so much about myself. I confided in you big-time, but you couldn't bring yourself to do the same, could you, Nicola?' His eyes were as icy as the deceptively blue autumn sky outside. 'When it came to the crunch, you just didn't trust me.'

His accusatory words stung her skin like tiny barbs and it took a moment or two before she could answer, her words sounding small. 'Maybe I don't trust anyone.'

'Well, what do you know?' he said sarcastically. 'Mutual distrust. Not much of a basis for anything, is it, Nicola?'

And suddenly Nicola was scared by all these twisty *feelings* which were rising to the surface inside her, like scum in a pan of boiling bones. How dared he take the upper hand—as if he'd done everything right and she'd done everything wrong? Maybe nothing had really changed since her childhood, because no matter what she said, or did, she always seemed to be condemned for it.

'I don't understand why you're reacting like this,' she said, her temper beginning to flare. 'Because a woman with a messy life was expressly what you *didn't* want. How many times did you tell me you liked me because I was cool and aloof? The ice-maiden image turned you on—admit it! My supposed mystique was one of the things which attracted you in the first place, and my composure is what made you realise I'd be a good bet to take to Tuscany. And yes, it ended up being more than that—but our relationship was never intended to last, was it, Alessio? You told me that, too—in no uncertain terms. You spelt it out very clearly that you didn't want marriage, or children—in fact, you didn't want *any* kind of commitment. Was I supposed to ruin our brief affair by dumping a load of unsavoury stuff on you, which you didn't need to know?'

Alessio shook his head, unable to shake off the disappointment which was pressing down on his shoulders like a leaden weight. He wondered how he could ever have doubted his instincts. Not just his instincts but his experience of women. He had thought she was too good to be true and he had been right. Well, he had heard her out. He had listened to the reasoning behind her behaviour and it was difficult not to feel some compassion for what she had told him. But that didn't change the fact that he felt betrayed by her, and, surprisingly, that hurt.

Why?

Because he had mistakenly imagined some sort of bond to be growing between them? Maybe. At times his feelings had been behaving like cells on a Petri dish—multiplying and expanding in all directions without any input from him. And that was something he hadn't expected. Or wanted. His lips hardened. Because this was the reality of relationships—subterfuge and manipulation, smoke and mirrors—and he didn't need it. He didn't *need* pain and he certainly didn't need *her*. His life was easier without any kind of emotional complication. It was as simple as that. A sudden sense of freedom washed over him and he expelled a long sigh of relief. What a lucky escape he'd had. And he wondered if she had any idea how effectively she'd shot herself in the foot.

'You didn't tell me anything until you had to, until your back was up against the wall,' he accused softly. 'I wonder, would I ever have discovered more if there hadn't been a medical emergency?'

'Who knows?' A pulse was hammering at the base of her throat. 'I suppose I imagined that sharing secrets was the precursor to deepening a relationship—but ours was always flailing around in the shallows, wasn't it, Alessio?'

But Alessio shook his head because getting into pointless debate was a time-suck, when the only thing which mattered was regaining his freedom. 'I'm glad your nephew is okay,' he said, unable to miss the faint flare of light in her grey eyes and—just in case she thought he was leading up to something equally tender-hearted—he curved his lips into a smile he knew to be cruel. Because, despite everything, he liked her and she had been through too much to waste any of her precious life pining over a man like him. Better she hated him than imagined she loved him. 'And I wish you every success in the future, Nicola,' he finished softly. 'Please believe that.'

But it was with an unexpected wrench of his heart that he forced himself to turn away from her shimmering blonde beauty and let himself out of the tiny apartment.

CHAPTER THIRTEEN

'*SOLD?*' NICOLA STARED at the glimmering bronze statue with a sense of uncertainty, before redirecting her disbelieving gaze towards Sergio. 'You mean, someone's bought it?'

'I do.' Her boss nodded, his lips twitching. 'That *is* what usually happens when something gets sold, Nicola.'

Dutifully, she offered an answering smile, telling herself that only a very stupid person would be sad to see the back of something which served as a daily reminder of the thing she was most missing. Not just the sex—though, of course, that was a pretty unforgettable part of it. No. A lump lodged in her throat. It was *him* she was missing most of all. Alessio. The brilliant chemist with the looks of a movie star. She'd tried telling herself it shouldn't be this hard to forget him, because he'd never been around that much. But he had always been a constant in her thoughts. If ever she'd felt low or wistful, it had been enough to conjure up the memory of his brilliant eyes and hard body, or something he'd said which had made her laugh. She had basked in the knowledge that he was part of her life and always looked forward to their next meeting.

Surely that emphasised the fact that theirs had never been a *real* relationship but simply a construct of transatlantic sex sessions. Yes, they had eaten dinner together and taken the occasional trip to the theatre or cinema and once, memorably, to Brighton, where they had walked along the pebbled beach and dodged the waves and she had confessed how much she'd always wanted to live beside the sea. But that shouldn't be enough to produce this intense level of heartache, which wouldn't seem to go away. She ought to be *glad* that the wretched bronze was finally leaving the gallery—and she could cut her ties to the Italian scientist for ever.

Even so, she was unable to quell the tiny splinter of hope which pierced her heart as she regarded her boss. 'Who's bought it?'

'Ross Fleming—a new client. Has a place by the sea in Cornwall. He wants it as a surprise for his wife, apparently.'

'Oh.' Her heart gave a lift-shaft plummet. 'How... nice.'

'It's being shipped out tomorrow—but he wants someone to supervise the installation and it's all a bit of a rush.' Sergio smiled in the manner of somebody just about to offer a huge bonus. 'You wouldn't mind going down to Cornwall, would you, Nicola? Tack on a couple of extra days and make a break of it, hmm? Put some colour back in your cheeks.'

Going to Cornwall was the last thing she felt like doing. She wanted to hunker down with a good book, or go and see Jago and watch him kick his chubby little legs in the bath. But Nicola recognised that Stacey was in the process of forging a deep relationship with her son as they prepared for his daddy's release and they needed to do that together, without her crowding them.

She gave a bright smile. Of course she would go. Sergio thought he was doing her a favour, and hadn't he been ultra-diplomatic for weeks now? Refusing to ask a single question about why Alessio di Bari had been so keen to get his hands on her address. He'd even resisted commenting on the unusual fact that she hadn't been able to sell a single painting since the Italian billionaire's departure.

Didn't she owe him?

Didn't she owe it to herself to get out of this rut and embrace what the world had to offer?

She packed a small case, took a stunningly scenic train journey along the Cornish Riviera and, after jumping in a cab, was driven to a low-key but unbelievably chic hotel, overlooking the blue-grey waves of the Atlantic. She showered, pinned up her hair, put on her working uniform of white shirt, black skirt, and matching jacket and slithered into the back of the taxi the hotel had ordered for her.

'You going up to Morwind, are you?' said the driver, when she gave him the address. 'Beautiful place. They say the sea views from there are the best in the county.'

'I'm looking forward to seeing it,' she answered politely, before lapsing into silence, because Nicola wasn't in the mood for conversation. She was trying very hard to compose herself for what lay ahead. Because the statue had been bought by a man for his wife and, stupidly, that hurt. How he must love her to have such an expensive piece shipped here, as a surprise. Suddenly she couldn't stop wondering whether she had sold herself short. Had she made herself too available to a man she'd always known would one day cast her aside?

But defining relationships in that way was insane. She hadn't been seduced beneath that gleaming bronze because she had *expected* anything from Alessio. She had done it because she hadn't been able to stop herself. Because he had consumed her senses in every way. Because she had adored him. Truth was, she still did. It wasn't *his* fault he didn't feel the same way. It wasn't anybody's fault. And even though her foolish heart was badly shattered she couldn't bring herself to regret a single second of it.

'Here you go,' said the driver, pulling up outside a large, contemporary clifftop house which somehow looked as if it had been there since the beginning of time. She could see at once what the driver had meant about the view, but it was more than that which made it beautiful. There was a sense of being close to the elements—of being part of the sea and the sky. As the cab drove away Nicola watched the swell of the crest-fringed waves and listened to them crashing on the rocks below.

But she couldn't stand there for ever. Time to meet the romantic Ross Fleming and, possibly, his wife.

Despite the modern architecture, there was an old-fashioned brass knocker. But her knock went unanswered for so long that Nicola wondered whether it could be heard in such a large house. She was just about to try again when suddenly the door opened and the sight which greeted her was so far off her scale of reality that she actually dropped her handbag and didn't bother picking it up as she stared into eyes as blue as a summer sea.

Alessio looked more casual than she'd ever seen him. His jeans were faded and a dark cashmere sweater clung softly to the honed definition of his torso. His hair was longer, too—ruffled ebony locks framing the slashed contours of his features, so that he had something of the pirate about him. But the blue eyes were exactly the same—brilliant and blazing and beautiful—and Nicola's first instinct was to cry and laugh all at the same time, because it was so incredibly good to see him.

But she didn't do either. She was too busy trying to stop herself from trembling. How *dare* he set up such a meeting? Was this intended to give him some sort of sadistic pleasure—extracting a cruel revenge for having deceived him? She set her mouth into what she hoped was a forbidding line, because he had hurt her once but he damned well wasn't going to get the chance to hurt her again.

'Is this some sort of set-up between you and Sergio?' she demanded coldly.

'Sergio knows nothing about it.'

'I'm looking for Ross Fleming.'

'I am Ross Fleming.'

'Really? I thought your name was Alessio di Bari.'

'Fleming is a pseudonym.'

'For the purchase of bronze statues, presumably?'

His sensual lips curved with the hint of a smile. 'Well, yes.'

She made herself say it and suddenly her cool mask slipped, because how could you remain composed while uttering words which felt as corrosive as battery fuel on your lips? 'For your *wife.*'

Alessio could see the incomprehension on her face and wondered whether his grand gesture might have failed spectacularly, particularly as the hurt in her eyes had been replaced by a growing anger. 'Nicola—'

'Have you brought me all the way out here to rub my nose in it?' she declared, giving a furious toss of her gleaming blonde head. 'You didn't waste any time, did you, Alessio? How long have you been married for? Did you find someone as soon as we'd split, or had there been someone in the background all along? Why, the ink must barely be dry on the certificate!'

From a purely aesthetic point of view, he thought how magnificent she looked when she was filled with rage, but suddenly Alessio realised he needed to act quickly if he wanted to appease her, and he did. He wanted that more than anything. 'Please, Nicola. The wind is strong. Come inside.'

'If you think I'm setting foot inside your house then you are very much mistaken. You really think I'm prepared to face your wife? What do you think I'm made of, Alessio, *stone*?'

On the contrary. Alessio swallowed. She was all magnificent creamy flesh and stormy grey eyes— and currently in the process of bending to retrieve her handbag from the step, presumably to ring for a cab to take her away as quickly as possible. And he realised then that half measures would get him no-where. If he wanted her, he had to lay it on the line. To tell her. She needed to know how he felt. About her. About them. Yet how did a man break the habit of a lifetime and begin to articulate feelings he'd never dared confront before?

He sucked in an unsteady breath. 'There is no

wife. The statue is for you, Nicola.' He paused. 'Only for you.'

She looked at him blankly. 'For me? What are you talking about?'

'I said it was for my wife and it is. But only if you are prepared to be my wife, for you are the only woman I would ever contemplate marrying. Because... I love you,' he said and suddenly his words were gruff. 'My clever, strong, proud, brave Nicola. I love you so very much.'

She was still eying him with frowning suspicion. 'Weren't you supposed to say that *before* you asked me to marry you?'

'I don't know what I am supposed to say!' he declared, lifting his hands in exasperation, in as vulnerable a moment as he'd ever shared with another person. 'Because you have thrown me into a state of confusion from the moment I first laid eyes on you. You are chaos theory personified! You fascinated me. Infuriated me. Intrigued me. I never knew where I was with you.'

'I know that,' she said woodenly, but there was no joy on her face—just that continued veiled look of suspicion. 'On some level I always knew that was my winning card and that's why I held onto it so tightly. You didn't want anything more than that.'

'You're right. I didn't. Until things started to change, without me expecting it. Without me even wanting it. I began to feel relaxed in your company,' he continued softly. 'To look in my diary to work out when next I could see you—but I forced myself to ration my time with you because I could not afford to let you become an addiction. But I was fighting a losing battle. And when I *did* rework my schedule in order to surprise you—you told me you were busy. Do you remember?'

'I was helping look after Jago that night.'

'Ah, Jago.' He nodded. 'That lucky little baby.'

'Lucky?'

'Ma, certo,' he said, with emphasis. 'To have an aunt like you. To battle for him. To help his young mother. That night when he was sick, my admiration of you knew no bounds. Do you realise that, Nicola? You didn't need to conceal anything about yourself, *cara mio*, because in that moment you were more amazing than I'd ever seen you.'

'You certainly weren't showing much admiration at the time,' she objected stubbornly.

Acknowledging her accusation, he nodded. *'Lo so.* I reacted badly because of the way you made me feel. Make me feel,' he corrected. 'Which is…'

Her grey gaze was steady, her features impassive. She was not helping him, he realised—and maybe that was a good thing.

'Scared,' he admitted at last. 'All my life I had vowed to never let anything scare me because for me that indicated weakness, which was a trait I could not tolerate. But I am living with that feeling now—

all the time—and there is only one way to rid myself of it. I have tried to forget you, Nicola, but that is impossible. I have tried to contemplate spending the rest of my life without you—but that is unthinkable. With you, I want all the things I never imagined wanting. To build a home. To have babies. But I still don't know how you feel about such a prospect.'

Still she didn't speak and he nodded, knowing he wasn't done yet—knowing he owed her more. 'I'm sorry for the way I behaved.'

She inclined her head. 'I was always taught that if someone offers an apology, then you must accept it.' She paused. 'But only if they really mean it.'

'From the very bottom of my heart.'

'Then I am sorry, too,' she said suddenly. 'I should have trusted you, but I was scared, too. I should have let you see that I loved you, but I was terrified you would reject me and push me away. Oh, Alessio.'

His heart was pounding as he asked her again. 'Does this mean you're going to marry me, Nicola Bennett?'

She glanced at the ground before looking up again and as he met her grey gaze he realised what she really wanted. And even though his scientific brain regarded such a desire with perplexity—bemusement, even—the man who loved her wanted it, too. For wasn't this the ultimate romantic gesture? Wasn't this what men had done since they first started losing their hearts to women? 'Marry me, *cara. Il mio unico grande amore,*' he said, as he dropped down onto one knee. 'My one and only love.'

And suddenly she was kneeling, too—not seeming to care about the damp step or the keen Atlantic breeze—and her arms were tight around his neck, her lips opening beneath his as she kissed him and kissed him, before breathing 'yes' into his mouth.

He wasn't really aware of the journey from the doorstep to the bedroom or how many items of clothing they dropped along the way, only that her stockings were ripped at the knees and he didn't feel complete until he had filled her with his seed. Quite literally. It was only afterwards that he realised it was the first time in his life he'd neglected to wear a condom.

'What if I've made you pregnant?' he demanded huskily.

Against his neck, Nicola giggled. 'Do you know, I think I'd be over the moon?'

'Me, too.' He gave an unsteady laugh. 'How crazy is that?'

'Totally crazy,' she agreed solemnly, turning to stare at the wide sweep of sea outside the window and thinking how beautiful it was. 'Why did you buy this house?'

'I haven't bought it—that would have been too presumptuous. I'm renting it, but it can be ours any time you want. You told me you didn't like skyscrapers and had always wanted to live by the sea, but we can live anywhere in the world. And, of course, we need to take your family into account.'

'My family?' she echoed tentatively.

He nodded. 'I can help your brother find work when he gets out of prison.'

'What sort of work? His CV is terrible!'

'He can learn a trade,' he said gently. 'He can find out what he's good at and use that. Because it's never too late to change. To start again. Or to fall in love. Life is whatever we choose to make it, Nicola—and I choose to make it with you.'

And suddenly she was crying, only this time he wasn't freaking out because she was displaying un-wanted emotion—he was drying her tears with his fingers and his lips. And he was crying, too.

EPILOGUE

THIS HOUSE WAS beautiful all year round, but Nicola loved it best in autumn. That was the time when the sun set straight in the west, dancing on the waves and flooding their bedroom with a rich, flame-coloured radiance. It was pouring in now, warming her skin and making it glow.

'Alessio?' she whispered, but he didn't answer and she shifted her position to glance down at her husband's sleeping form, wondering if life could get any more perfect. She smiled. Actually, yes, she suspected it could…

For almost three years now, they had been spending weekends in their beautiful Cornish home, following their London wedding. In an intimate ceremony, they had married in Marylebone register office with a small reception at the Ritz Hotel. It had seemed, as Alessio had whispered to her, an appropriate place to begin married life. They had honeymooned in Italy—touring the art-studded cities of

Florence, Siena and Rome, which Nicola had always longed to visit.

But Alessio had surprised her yet again. He had taken her to the tiny mountain village where he'd lived with his grandmother and where he had retained his *nonna*'s tiny apartment above the bakery, having it religiously cleaned and maintained every week. They had spent two nights there—time enough for Nicola to experience the place he had come from, which he had left so long ago. But people in the street recognised him, and smiled—and the newly-weds lit a candle in the tiny church, where they had their vows blessed by the local priest. And maybe it was seeing their shining smiles of nuptial contentment in the photo Alessio sent to his mother which encouraged her to leave her mockery of a marriage at last. After a lot of thought, she had gone back to live in Italy, to Lecce—and they now visited her there, at least once a year.

Despite knowing she could branch out on her own, Nicola had continued to work for Sergio. She didn't want the hassle of starting up a new business and wasn't sure she had the necessary entrepreneurial streak. She was far more interested in devoting time to her precious marriage. Meanwhile, Alessio had opened his first English factory, which had brought so much employment to an impoverished section of the country.

Hearing a yawn and a contented sigh from beside

her, Nicola looked down to meet the brilliance of her husband's gaze. 'You sound satisfied,' she remarked.

'That's because I am. You are very good at satisfying a man, *cara*.' He smiled and gave another lazy yawn, his gaze raking over her. 'It's good to be on our own again. Much as though I enjoyed the weekend.'

'So did I. Jago is so adorable, and Callum's so contented. Why, he's hardly recognisable as the same person. Even Stacey said so.'

'He has lost his prison pallor,' Alessio said suddenly. 'He has grown into a strong man.'

'And all thanks to you, my love.'

Because Alessio had helped her brother on his release from prison, getting him an apprenticeship as a cabinetmaker, the exquisite carvings he had made in jail pointing him firmly in the direction of his new career. Callum had married Stacey and they'd moved into a pretty cottage in Somerset, with a huge garden for little Jago to run around in. A place to keep chickens and grow vegetables and to live a quiet, rural life. It wasn't a life the young couple had ever anticipated, but it filled them with utter joy.

Yes, everything was good—more than good. Their only disappointment was that Nicola hadn't become pregnant. But they both had tried to keep this in perspective and count their many other blessings. Alessio had mentioned fostering, or adoption, or neither—if that was what they decided.

'What are you looking so pensive about, *mio cara*?'

The velvety voice beside her was curious, but Nicola closed her eyes, not wanting her expression to give her away. Wanting to savour her news for a few wonderful seconds more.

'I was just thinking—'

'Dangerous,' he murmured, her lashes fluttering open as his finger moved slowly down the side of her cheek. 'It wouldn't have anything to do with a baby, would it, *cara mio*? More specifically, *our* baby?'

She blinked at him, amazement and happiness written all over her face. 'How on earth did you know?'

Alessio smiled. He could list the physical signs of her condition, which had subtly changed a body he knew and loved so well. The slight tenderness of her breasts and almost imperceptible softening of her belly. With his scientific eye for detail, he had observed her refusing a bowl of figs for breakfast, which usually she adored. Her hair was even shinier, too.

But the reason behind his conclusion was simple. It was based on a principle which gave them both endless pleasure whenever he expressed it. His lips curved into a smile as he pulled her down into his arms.

'Because I love you,' he said.

* * * * *

Swept away by Italian Nights to Claim the Virgin?
*Then lose yourself in these other passionate
stories by Sharon Kendrick!*

Confessions of His Christmas Housekeeper
Penniless and Pregnant in Paradise
Stolen Nights with the King
Her Christmas Baby Confession
Innocent Maid for the Greek

Available now!

#4117 HER VOW TO BE HIS DESERT QUEEN
Three Ruthless Kings
by Jackie Ashenden

Khalil ibn Amir al-Nazari never forgot the marriage pact innocent Sidonie Sullivan scribbled on a napkin five years ago. Now, he'll enforce it to save his kingdom! But can he convince Sidonie that he wants her for herself too?

#4118 PREGNANT AT THE PALACE ALTAR
Secrets of the Kalyva Crown
by Lorraine Hall

King Diamandis finds solace in hard facts and duty. So, after a reckless night of abandon results in two heirs, marriage is nonnegotiable! The challenge is convincing his former assistant, Katerina Floros, to see that too...

#4119 HER DIAMOND DEAL WITH THE CEO
by Louise Fuller

When lifeguard Ondine rescues Jack Walcott from drowning, she almost regrets it. The billionaire is as rude and entitled as he is gorgeous, so Ondine doesn't expect any thanks. And certainly not his convenient marriage proposal!

#4120 ONE NIGHT IN MY RIVAL'S BED
by Melanie Milburne

Grayson Barlowe's always been my enemy, yet I've never been immune to his devilish good looks. We were taught to compete on the business battlefield. Now, working together requires a truce that has landed me in the place I vowed I'd never be—*between his sheets!*

YOU CAN FIND MORE INFORMATION ON UPCOMING HARLEQUIN TITLES, FREE EXCERPTS AND MORE AT HARLEQUIN.COM.

HPCNMRB0523

Get 3 FREE REWARDS!

We'll send you 2 FREE Books plus a FREE Mystery Gift.

FREE Value Over **$20**

Both the **Harlequin®** **Desire** and **Harlequin Presents®** series feature compelling novels filled with passion, sensuality and intriguing scandals.

YES! Please send me 2 FREE novels from the Harlequin Desire or Harlequin Presents series and my FREE gift (gift is worth about $10 retail). After receiving them, if I don't wish to receive any more books, I can return the shipping statement marked "cancel." If I don't cancel, I will receive 6 brand-new Harlequin Presents Larger-Print books every month and be billed just $6.30 each in the U.S. or $6.49 each in Canada, a savings of at least 10% off the cover price, or 3 Harlequin Desire books (2-in-1 story editions) every month and be billed just $7.83 each in the U.S. or $8.43 each in Canada, a savings of at least 12% off the cover price. It's quite a bargain! Shipping and handling is just 50¢ per book in the U.S. and $1.25 per book in Canada.* I understand that accepting the 2 free books and gift places me under no obligation to buy anything. I can always return a shipment and cancel at any time by calling the number below. The free books and gift are mine to keep no matter what I decide.

Choose one: ☐ **Harlequin Desire** (225/326 BPA GRNA) ☐ **Harlequin Presents Larger-Print** (176/376 BPA GRNA) ☐ **Or Try Both!** (225/326 & 176/376 BPA GRQP)

Name (please print)

Address   Apt. #

City   State/Province   Zip/Postal Code

Email. Please check this box ☐ if you would like to receive newsletters and promotional emails from Harlequin Enterprises ULC and its affiliates. You can unsubscribe anytime.

> **Mail to the Harlequin Reader Service:**
> **IN U.S.A.:** P.O. Box 1341, Buffalo, NY 14240-8531
> **IN CANADA:** P.O. Box 603, Fort Erie, Ontario L2A 5X3
>
> Want to try 2 free books from another series! Call 1-800-873-8635 or visit www.ReaderService.com.

*Terms and prices subject to change without notice. Prices do not include sales taxes, which will be charged (if applicable) based on your state or country of residence. Canadian residents will be charged applicable taxes. Offer not valid in Quebec. This offer is limited to one order per household. Books received may not be as shown. Not valid for current subscribers to the Harlequin Presents or Harlequin Desire series. All orders subject to approval. Credit or debit balances in a customer's account(s) may be offset by any other outstanding balance owed by or to the customer. Please allow 4 to 6 weeks for delivery. Offer available while quantities last.

Your Privacy Your information is being collected by Harlequin Enterprises ULC, operating as Harlequin Reader Service. For a complete summary of the information we collect, how we use this information and to whom it is disclosed, please visit our privacy notice located at corporate.harlequin.com/privacy-notice. From time to time we may also exchange your personal information with reputable third parties. If you wish to opt out of this sharing of your personal information, please visit readerservice.com/consumerschoice or call 1-800-873-8635. Notice to California Residents—Under California law, you have specific rights to control and access your data. For more information on these rights and how to exercise them, visit corporate.harlequin.com/california-privacy.

HDHP23

HARLEQUIN
PLUS

Try the best multimedia subscription service for romance readers like you!

Read, Watch and Play.

Experience the easiest way to get the romance content you crave.

Start your **FREE TRIAL** at
<u>www.harlequinplus.com/freetrial</u>.